D1437325

IN THE ABSENCE
OF MRS. PETERSEN

Also by
NIGEL BALCHIN

★

LIGHTBODY ON LIBERTY
DARKNESS FALLS FROM THE AIR
THE SMALL BACK ROOM
MINE OWN EXECUTIONER
LORD, I WAS AFRAID
THE BORGIA TESTAMENT
A SORT OF TRAITORS
THE ANATOMY OF VILLAINY
A WAY THROUGH THE WOOD
SUNDRY CREDITORS
LAST RECOLLECTIONS OF MY UNCLE CHARLES
THE FALL OF THE SPARROW
SEEN DIMLY BEFORE DAWN

IN THE ABSENCE
OF MRS. PETERSEN

★

NIGEL BALCHIN

THE COMPANION BOOK CLUB
LONDON

© Nigel Balchin, 1966

This edition is issued by arrangement
with William Collins, Sons & Co. Ltd.

The Thane of Fife, had a wife: where is she now?

*Made and printed in Great Britain
for the Companion Book Club (Odhams Books Ltd.)
by Odhams (Watford) Limited
Watford, Herts.*
S.767.UC.

THERE was an article in a magazine the other day, pointing out the remarkable safety of present-day air travel. According to the writer, statistics show that there is a greater chance of being kicked to death by a mule, or of dying of laughter in the theatre, than of being killed in an air accident.

Properly selected and carefully trained statistics often show some very odd things. No really close acquaintance of mine has ever been kicked to death by a mule. Perhaps I live in the wrong part of the world. I have never been in a theatre when anybody has died of laughter. Perhaps I don't go to the right plays. But I was present when Flight 265 left Los Angeles International Airport for New York, and since then, except for one brief period, I have been very much alone.

§

There are people who like living in Hollywood—or, as they more frequently do, in Beverly Hills or the San Fernando Valley. They like that monotonous sunshine, and the house with the swimming-pool, and the hut on the beach, and the curious illusion of earning a lot of money, and settle down perfectly happily to live the rest of their lives there, and presumably to be buried at Forest Lawn. But for me it has always been purely a working place—somewhere to go to do a specific job, and then to come away from, with no further criticisms on either side. Living there, I have always felt like a man driving a car at night with all his lights on, and all his electrical equipment working. A lot is going out, mentally speaking, and very little is coming in; and after a few months of it, one must go away and drive the car somewhere else in daylight, in order to recharge the batteries.

I had never thought that Sarah would like Hollywood. I even tried, admittedly rather feebly, to prevent her from coming with me. If you are working all day, particularly if you have been lucky enough to get decent, clever, and interesting people to work with, the life is just possible. But if you are simply somebody's wife, living there for a few months in a luxurious furnished apartment, it must be desperately difficult to get through the time. And Sarah was never very good at doing nothing.

Yet when she finally struck, I was strangely unprepared for it. We had only been in the place two months, during which I had been fully occupied in doing my first rapid draft of a script in which I was interested. To me, the really heart-breaking part of a scriptwriter's work—the meetings with the Front Office, the gradual tearing away of all distinction from what one has written, the fatuous suggestions which have to be treated politely and respectfully, and the eventual realization that you are talking a completely different language—all these had yet to come. We had acquired the usual beach-hut at Malibu. We had duly been to Disneyland, and down across the border into Mexico; and we had only been about four times each to all the obvious restaurants. This, so far, was the classical Hollywood assignment.

It was also part of the classical assignment that we should go that evening to Barry Fowler's party. Barry was the executive producer of the picture on which I was working. He was a well-known figure in Hollywood, with an excellent record of productions—a big, rather portly grey-haired man, with excellent manners, who prided himself chiefly on his taste in such things as French wine and English clothes. He had just married a new wife (his fourth, I fancy) who was very beautiful and some thirty years younger than he was, and had built her a new house. Hence the party.

The house was a huge affair right up at the top of one of the canyons, perched on the edge of a mountain, so that it looked as though at any moment it might slide down, complete with the swimming-pool, into Beverly Hills. It was one of those places where, as you look at the view, they tell you that on a clear day you can see Marine Land or something. On these occasions it never *is* a clear day, and this one wasn't; but even so the view was magnificent, and I am quite prepared to believe that on a *really* clear day one could see Japan.

There were about thirty people at the party, every one of whom, as far as I know, was connected with the film industry in some capacity or other. They included half a dozen top ranking film-stars, several directors and producers, and a world-famous Funny Man of television, who had become so used to being a Funny Man that he could not stop, even in private life. Altogether, by Hollywood standards, it was a very distinguished gathering. It would have been a splendid opportunity for any keen autograph hunter.

Unfortunately neither Sarah nor I were keen autograph hunters, and from the outset it was clear that the whole party was not going to be quite our cup of tea. We all went and looked at the view and agreed that it was marvellous and that on a clear day et cetera et cetera. We then had to go and look at the new house. The only

7

thing I remember about it with any clarity is a bathroom whose walls were of white buttoned leather, with gold washbasin and taps, and an enormous sort of glass showcase completely filled with the new Mrs. Fowler's various brands of scent. Next to it was Mrs. Fowler's bedroom which had in it a bed at least twelve feet wide. When you pressed the appropriate button the bed tilted up to an accommodating angle, and shutters slid back to reveal a large television set. Sarah whispered in my ear, 'I suppose if they're both sleeping in that bed, and want to get together, they make an appointment by telephone to meet in the middle.'

The most entertaining thing about looking at the house was the performance of Miss Mary Gladstone. Miss Gladstone has, if I recall the figures correctly, a bust of forty-eight inches, and she made at that time the sort of pictures that called for a bust of forty-eight inches. She was wearing a frock which looked as though it had been put on with a spray gun. There were very few stairs in Barry's new house, but in that frock there was no question of Miss Gladstone being able to walk up or down stairs, so that when she came to any stairs she simply stood and spread her arms out, and her escort, a vast young man, picked her up and carried her up or down to the next level, as one might carry up or down anybody in an invalid chair. I don't know how she came to be there at all, since whatever else Barry is, he certainly is a snob. But it was quite obvious from the attitude of the rest of the guests that Miss Gladstone and her escort would not do. I had never realized before that there are class distinctions amongst film-stars, but I did notice that the other well-known stars present, though greeting one another rapturously, cut Miss Gladstone dead. The party went on along the usual lines, except that the English butler whom everybody always hired for these occasions,

8

and who was now getting very old and frail, had a tray of champagne elbowed out of his hands, and some of it went over the dress of a very famous star indeed. Apart from this one moment of excitement, everybody rhapsodized for a few minutes about Barry's new house, and then, with an almost audible sigh of relief, turned to the proper subject of Hollywood conversation—the film they had just made, or were making, or were about to make. I noticed that Sarah seemed to be making rather heavy weather of the whole thing. She was standing talking to —or rather being talked to by—my agent, Joe Luce. Sarah could not abide Joe Luce, and she was half pretending to listen as she stood looking round the room with her head haughtily raised, and an expression on her face that implied that she could smell a dead rat under the floor boards. Even so, I could not help noticing that despite the presence of four major female stars, Miss Gladstone, Barry's new wife, and a dozen other people whose job it was to be decorative, she was still by far the most beautiful and attractive woman in the room.

After about an hour we were all herded into the television room, to see the Funny Man's latest programme. He gave us a running commentary on it as it was shown, and everybody laughed very heartily indeed. For myself I couldn't make up my mind whether he was even less funny in real life than on the screen, or vice versa. The programme lasted half an hour, and it seemed longer. After it, we all went back again to the usual subject of conversation, and Barry took me across and introduced me to Miss Mary Gladstone. It was the first time I had ever talked to anybody with a forty-eight inch bust in a very low cut frock, and I found it slightly embarrassing. Miss Gladstone was a platinum blonde with forget-me-not blue eyes. She was a pleasant enough, rather simple girl with an attractive childish grin, and we talked, I fancy, about England and the film that she had recently made there. But try as I might to rivet my eyes on hers, I simply could not prevent my glance from flickering downwards occasionally to the famous bosom, jutting out so largely, nakedly and to me repulsively, under my very nose.

However, there we were, Miss Gladstone and I, having quite a pleasant conversation and harming none, when she turned away for a moment to speak to somebody else, and immediately Sarah was by my side and positively hissing in my ear, 'For God's sake sober up. You're making an absolute fool of yourself.'

I said, 'What do you mean, sober up? I'm not drunk.'

'You are. You can hardly stand.'

I do not like champagne, and I had drunk precisely one and a half glasses of it, but from experience, I at once knew the form. For Sarah to accuse me of being drunk at a party simply meant that she was hating the whole thing and wanted to go home. I was slightly irritated, as I always was by this particular technique, and I said, 'In exactly what way am I making a fool of myself?'

'You keep on looking down the front of that ghastly creature's frock.'

'Darling, if you're talking to her, there's nowhere else to look. You try, and you'll see what I mean.'

Sarah said, 'Then why talk to her? Nobody else does. Anyhow, I'll leave you to it. Personally, I'm going home.'

Before I had time to say anything she had turned to Barry's new wife, held out her hand and said, 'Good-bye. Thank you for a lovely party. I'm green with envy about your house,' and started for the door.

There was nothing to do but follow her, since apart from anything else she had no keys to the car and no means of getting home. As we got into the car I said, 'Sarah dear, I do wish you'd cut out that particular act.'

'What act?'

'Trying to start a row with me just because you're bored. Admittedly it wasn't exactly my idea of a good party, but that wasn't my fault.'

Sarah said, 'Well, what *I* wish is that you wouldn't embarrass me in public.'

I sighed and said, 'Now what on earth did I do that could possibly have embarrassed you?'

'Getting drunk and then picking up some tart and leering at her.'

'You know perfectly well that I wasn't drunk. I didn't pick up the Gladstone girl—or the Gladstone bag if you like that better. Barry introduced me to her. And I certainly wasn't aware that I was leering at her. We were having a perfectly innocent conversation about England, and as a matter of fact she's quite a nice girl, even if she has got a forty-eight inch bust.'

This was received in sulky silence. As we drove down the canyon, I decided to have a shot at putting things right. I put out my hand and took hers and said, 'Anyhow, what have you got to nark about, partner? You were by far the most attractive woman in the room.'

Sarah said, 'Don't be ridiculous. I'm pounds overweight, and all my clothes are too tight.'

'They're not as tight as most of the other women's. I should think they have to use a blow lamp to get the Gladstone girl out of hers.'

Sarah gave a sort of little giggle and said, 'Melted off her and then use a scraper, eh?'

I said, 'That's right,' and knew that for once these overtures were being accepted. There was a pause, and then she said in a small voice:

'I'm sorry, Jim.'

And I said, 'Forget it, honey. Anyhow, it's got us away from a pretty awful party.'

We said no more until we reached the house. Sarah went straight into the bedroom, and I followed. I went and put my arms round her and kissed her and undid the zip at the back of her frock and slipped it off her shoulders so that she could wriggle it down over her hips. I said, 'There you are, you see—no blow lamp necessary.'

She stood there for a moment in her brassière and pantie belt and stockings, with the frock in a heap around her ankles, and then she stepped out of the frock and threw it carelessly on the bed, and put her arms round my neck and kissed me silently and very hard. And that, for the moment, was that.

Yet the following morning, before we had even drunk our morning coffee and eaten the dollar wheat-cakes with maple syrup, Sarah said, 'Jim—how much longer are you going to have to stay here?'

I said, 'On present form, and if Barry can carry the Front Office with him, probably two months. Can't be much less, and if we strike a snag, maybe longer. A lot depends on what happens this afternoon. Barry and I are seeing Gloag. Barry's perfectly happy with the script. But if Gloag suddenly decides that the whole thing ought to happen in eighteenth-century Vienna, or that the girl's part ought really to be played by Frank Sinatra, it'll take longer. Don't worry, darling. If they haven't got what they want out of me within six months, they'll fire me anyway, and then we shall be able to go home.'

'You mean it could be another four months?'

'Could be.'

There was a long pause while she looked, not at me, but at the corner of the room, with those curious big, grey-green eyes, and then she turned to me and with that upward tilt of the chin which I knew so well said, 'Darling—I think I've had this place. I don't think I can do any more of it.'

'Bored?'

'Worse than bored. The place has a sort of . . . of *deadening* thing about it . . . Jim—can't we just pack it in and go home now?'

I was mildly irritated and said, 'Well, obviously *I* can't. I've contracted to do this job and I must do it. Anyhow, if I bowed out now it would cost us about 50,000 dollars.'

'Damn the 50,000 dollars.'

'That's all very well, my dear, but you'll be glad enough to spend them.'

'Well, anyhow,' said Sarah sullenly, 'I'm warning you that I can't take any more of this. I've got to get away from here or I shall go out of my mind.'

'Try going down to the beach for a few days.'

'I hate that place. It smells. And what with the traffic on Pacific Highway and the noise of the sea, I can't sleep there.'

'All right then—go home.'

'Not without you.'

I said, 'I'm sorry, Sarah, but I did warn you that you wouldn't like it. If you don't want to stay here, and don't want to go to the beach, and don't want to go home alone, what *do* you want to do?'

It was a silly, point-scoring question, because I knew perfectly well that Sarah in this mood would have no idea what she really wanted. We sat in glum silence for a few moments and then I relented and said, 'How about going to New York for a few days? You always like New York.'

Her head came up and her face brightened. She said, 'New York . . . ?' thoughtfully, and I knew that that was the answer.

I said, 'Well, think it over. I've got to go to the studio now.'

13

Whatever else they don't do for writers in Hollywood, they do at least usually give you a comfortable office which is quiet, and a reasonably efficient secretary. I have often thought that writing conditions at most of the big studios would be ideal—if there were anything to write. My office had the usual couch on which one presumably lies and thinks great big thoughts. I lay on mine and tried to work out what Gloag would probably say about the draft script, and what Barry and I ought to say in reply. I did not altogether trust Barry in this party. He was a nice man, and we had got on well together. But I knew from bitter experience that very few Hollywood producers will stick to their guns and back up their writer, if the Front Office happens to be critical.

About twelve o'clock, Sarah called me. She said, 'Darling—I've taken you at your word. I'm going to New York. Are you sure you'll be all right?'

I said, 'Sure. When are you going?'

'Well . . . late this afternoon. Five o'clock.'

'You haven't wasted much time.'

'Jim darling—I'm sorry, and I know it's awful of me. But you can't think how important it is to me to get away. If you don't think you'll be all right alone, of course I won't go. . . .'

'Nonsense. Of course you must go. Anyhow it'll give me a chance to do a bit of blonde-chasing. I might even look up the Gladstone bag. Where are you going to stay in New York?'

'With Martha. I called her, and she made all those warm American noises. I shan't stay more than a week.'

'Well, that's all right. Have a good time, darling.'

'Will you come and see me off?'

14

'At five o'clock? Don't know if I can make it. Depends how long we take with Gloag. But I'll come if I possibly can. Got any money?'

'I've still got all my travellers' cheques.'

'They won't last too long in New York. Still—in case I don't make it, have a good time, darling. Call me when you get there.'

§

We were supposed to see Frank Gloag at two. We saw him eventually at three o'clock, by which time he had loosened his tie, undone his collar, and was in his best script-wrecking mood. He walked up and down his office smoking Panatellas, and explaining to us with the greatest charm and courtesy what the story was really about, and how to write it. His views on these things almost ignored the book that I had been given to adapt, and in the next hour he made fourteen suggestions, of which two were extremely good, two usable at a pinch, and the other ten quite unusable unless we started again from scratch.

At about four-thirty, I said, 'Frank . . .' (I had been carefully taught that, 'this is a first-name studio') 'Frank . . . you realize that if your central character *isn't* a sick man when the picture opens, then we have no story? After all, that's what the book's about.'

Gloag waved a hand and said, 'Oh, to hell with the book, Jim. I never liked it anyway. It's a down-beat story. Listen—if you boys can get this right, I might be able to get Burt Lancaster for you.'

I said, 'I'd never thought of Charles as being a Burt Lancaster part. I thought of him as being about twenty-five.'

Barry said, with almost breathless admiration, 'Burt would be a wonderful idea, Frank.'

15

Gloag said, 'Of course he would. Well, you boys work out something along those lines. I've got somebody coming in now.' He clapped me on the shoulder and said, 'Jim boy, you're doing a wonderful job. You can lick this.'

§

When we came out of Gloag's office I glanced at my watch, and realized that to get to the airport by five was probably not on, but only just not on. Barry started to say, 'I think there is a lot in what Frank says. . . .'

I said, 'There's a hell of a lot in what he says. Let's talk about it to-morrow,' and legged it across to the car-park.

I should have made it, if I had known what line and what flight she was going on, but I hadn't asked her, and by the time I'd checked this at the desks, the gates were closed and the big jet carrying the Fifth Avenue Express passengers was out on the runway, ready to go. There was nothing to do but to go up to the flight-deck and watch her off. I remember being worried in case Sarah should think that I hadn't come to see her off because I was cross with her about going to New York, which I honestly wasn't. I also remember the flight-deck with great vividness, with its flags of all the nations fluttering, and a small boy with a lot of freckles, who was using the big binoculars, and talking to his mother, who stood beside him. There was a jack rabbit too, who suddenly bunked across the in-field. Then the big jet for New York went down the runway, and I think I said, 'God bless you, you silly old thing.' Then the right wing dipped and seemed to hit the runway, and the whole thing turned into a sort of gigantic catherine-wheel, which rolled over and over, throwing flaming bits off itself, and what was left came to rest with a curious jarring sound which, from the flight-deck, sounded no more than as though somebody in a car had put on his brakes rather suddenly. After that it was all flames and smoke and people rushing past with white faces. The freckled boy who had the binoculars turned slowly away from them with the freckles standing out on his face in a fantastic pattern. He said, 'Oh, Mummy . . . Oh, Mummy . . .' and started to cry. Within seconds the crash-wagons and the fire engines were tearing across the aerodrome, and people even started to run from somewhere towards the flames and smoke. But what the hell was the use? It was two miles away.

★ 2 ★

MY recollections of the next two or three days are just vivid flashes in a void. When I was young I used to play a lot of cricket, and I remember that when I was out, there was always a moment when I wondered, with desperate hope, whether the umpire might have called a no-ball, and that therefore I should have survived. In something of the same spirit, I must have gone down and looked at the passenger list, to make sure that she had really been aboard, because I remember that on it she appeared as 'Mrs. S. Peterson,' whereas I had always told her that her proper name was Mrs. James Petersen. Then there was the studio. I can't remember much about Barry but I can remember Frank ('This is a first-name studio') Gloag saying, 'Just a moment, Jim boy,' and going away and coming back with a whisky, and thinking that it was a very large, dark whisky, and thinking how extremely uselessly kind everybody was being. I know I went to the bank and drew 40,000 dollars, because I remember thinking how much less fuss they make in an American bank when you're drawing money out than when you're putting money in. If you want to pay 20,000 dollars into an American bank, they very nearly need to see your birthmarks and to know your mother's maiden name, before they'll accept it. But after that, if you want to draw the complete balance of your account, it takes you half a minute.

Apart from that, the person who arranged everything,

of course, was Joe Luce, my agent—the one that Sarah had always so strongly and irrationally disliked. In Hollywood, your agent takes ten per cent of what you make, which can be a lot of money. But on the other hand, if he is a good agent, he certainly earns it, because he not only finds you work, represents you in negotiations, goes in to bat for you in any argument and so on, but also acts as a sort of universal aunt, who finds you houses, hires you cars, and comes and bails you out if you find yourself in gaol for drunken driving. During the first few days after the crash, when I was in a zombie-like state of shock, it was Joe Luce who arranged everything—explaining to the studio that I obviously could not go on with the picture, closing down the house and the beach hut, paying my bills, getting rid of the car, and so on. Everything that Joe could do for me in these practical matters was done. There were only a few things which not even the best agent can do for his client, and these were the ones I chiefly remember.

There was the question, for example, of what to do with the things that Sarah had left in the house. Although she had said she was only going for a week, she had taken with her most of her best clothes, and practically all her jewellery. But even so, there was half a cupboard full of assorted clothes, odd pairs of slacks, and a couple of cotton dresses, a drawer full of rather battered underclothes and nightdresses, and a box with two or three not very valuable rings, a rather fine antique bracelet that I had bought her in Florence, and a pair of sapphire ear-rings, which I had given her on her last birthday, and which for some reason she had never liked and never wore. There were also twenty-two pairs of shoes (Sarah always had a weakness for shoes) and lots of other things like nearly empty bottles of scent, and her camera, and a pair of sun-glasses, and God knows what else. I don't think anything else brought home to me so clearly that she was dead as this collection of ridiculous female possessions. They seemed to have a certain smell about them—a smell that I should never smell again, and when Joe asked me gently what I wanted done with them I remember almost screaming at him, 'Get rid of them! I don't care what you do with them as long as they're gone and forgotten.'

Two days later there was nothing in the house to remind me of Sarah. I have never known what Joe did with the things but bless him, he got rid of them, and I have sometimes wondered who is now wearing those sapphire ear-rings that Sarah never liked.

Then there was the identification parade, and here again there was nothing much that Joe could do for me. One would have thought that nothing could have survived in that flaming wreck, but apparently a certain number of things must have been flung out as the plane cartwheeled, and we, the next of kin of those killed in the crash, were bidden to come and claim what was left to us. I think it was Joe who persuaded me to go to this remarkable function, and who came with me. The things were all spread out on a counter such as customs officers use and carefully numbered, and there were some things like quite splendid air-line baggage which had survived practically untouched. Then there were things that had been badly singed or broken, and finally there were a lot of small things, like a pocket hip flask or children's toys. I remember particularly that there was one of those clock-work mice that run round tables and never fall off them, and recalling the old saying about the chance of a celluloid mouse being chased by an asbestos cat through hell. This mouse had been chased through hell and survived. But there was nothing in the whole display that might conceivably have belonged to Sarah, and this was something of a relief. If she was to be gone, I wanted her gone utterly and completely, without sentimental relics.

I didn't go to the mass funeral for the victims of the crash. I remember saying to Barry, 'Hell, why should I go to the funeral? They were decently cremated, weren't they? Sarah always wanted to be cremated.' Except for these few occasional moments I have no very clear recollections of a period which must have been about a week, but I think I must have gone through it fairly sensibly in a numb sort of way, doing what Joe told me I must do, and only longing desperately for the day when I could get away. I don't think that in the whole of this time I ever really thought clearly about Sarah, except when I found her passport when I was clearing up the house. From the moment I had seen that catherine-wheel of a plane on the runway at Los Angeles, I had known that she was dead; and with her there died a part of me, leaving me utterly free and utterly empty. What was I supposed to do about it? Burst into tears, like the freckled kid with the binoculars? All that tremendous vitality—that gust for things—that wish for the front seat everywhere—that generosity—that bitter criticism of everything and everybody—that intolerance and hatred —that nobleness and meanness—that essential femininity with no loyalty to anything but itself, now no more than a handful of indeterminate ashes, which were probably in somebody else's suitcase anyway. Rest you, sweetheart. You were pretty average hell, but you were the best and most generous girl in bed that I have ever known.

§

I reckoned it out the other day, and I must have flown, in all, about one hundred and fifty thousand miles in the last ten years. I once came the last five hundred miles over the Pacific to San Francisco on three engines, and I once cut my shins very badly on the seat in front when we hit a real wind-pocket coming into Shannon. That's the worst that has ever happened to me. Yet to this day I am frightened of flying, and would do almost anything to avoid it. It is all right if you are in practice. I once flew from Japan to Italy without turning a hair. People who are flying all the time think nothing of it—and neither do I once I get to the airport and see the crew and the stewardesses and the rest of the passengers. Everything is so under control that it seems as though nothing could go wrong. And yet—and yet—and yet . . . ? Why wasn't I there to hold her hand when that wing dipped? Dexterous, surprisingly cold hand. I wonder if she was frightened too, in a plane that was taking off? I expect so. To be frightened is feminine, and she never lost a chance of being feminine. But you weren't frightened, my love, were you, when that wing dipped? The wing just dipped and you were dead. That's the answer, isn't it? And of course, I shall be all right by myself. Chance for some blonde-chasing.

§

Then I was walking up the ramp into an aircraft, and being shown to my seat by the stewardess, and saying to myself all the time, 'If you don't fly now, you'll never fly again.' 'If you don't fly now, you'll never fly again. . . .' I don't think I knew where the plane was going, but it was going somewhere, and that was all right with me. I think I must have been rather drunk. I remember that Barry and Joe had seen me off with that air of careful mourning which the whole studio had adopted, though why the hell they should care whether Sarah was alive or dead defeats me.

Anyhow, we taxied out to our take-off point, four times

ran our engines up to make sure they were working, and each time I thought we were taking-off and died the cindery death. Then suddenly my seat hit me in the middle of the back, and we were launched along the runway, and I put out my hand and there was no rather surprisingly cold hand to take mine, and after that I didn't mind what happened. I remember that as we were airborne I said, as I always do when taking-off, 'Into thy hands, O Lord, I commend my spirit.' But it was no more than a formula. For once in my life I was not frightened at taking-off in an aeroplane. There was nothing left to be frightened of now.

§

When we got to the other end it turned out to be Chicago. Presumably I must have booked myself to Chicago, or got somebody else to do it for me, but I have no recollection of it, nor any idea why I went there. I have a vague recollection of going to the Arts Institute and of reflecting, as I had often done before, that it is possible to have too many Renoirs.

But by the following day things began to come a little more into focus. There was a bitter wind blowing off Lake Michigan, and that may have helped. I went into a café to get out of it, and there, for the first time since the wing had dipped, I began to think, slowly and carefully, but at least coherently. The facts, I decided, were that Sarah's plane to New York crashed and so she was dead, and my plane to Chicago had not crashed and therefore I was alive. This was the one contingency that I had never reckoned with. I had spent a good deal of time worrying about what would happen to Sarah if I died, but I had never for a moment considered what would happen to me if she died. One of my first realizations was that I now could not, as I had intended to do, give her a fur coat for her birthday. I had always loved giving her presents, and the realization that I could no longer give her presents came as a bitter blow. I worked back from that to a lot of other things which would now not happen or be quite pointless. We had promised ourselves that when we returned from this Hollywood trip, we would buy a small place on the Italian Riviera. There was the flat in London. The whole decoration and furnishing of it made it entirely Sarah's place, not mine. I certainly didn't want to live there alone. My life was insured for thirty thousand pounds—now for no obvious reason. My total assets were about seventy thousand pounds and what the hell did I want with seventy thousand pounds? And above all there was that big bed at the flat—the only really comfortable bed in the world—and now there was nobody to lie in a heap with.

I added it all up, quite calmly and coldly, and it seemed to come to nought point nought nought recurring. I had just reached this answer when somebody—I think he must have been the manager of the café—paused at my table and said, 'Cheer up, boy. Do you know anybody who has as good a time as folks?' I think it must have been a stock line of his, which he always used when he saw anybody looking serious. Anyhow, he passed on before I could think of a suitable reply, and I suddenly realized that it was really no use sitting in a café in Chicago. Decisions had to be taken about this whole business of being alive.

The one thing I was quite sure about was that it couldn't be London. In London there would be her clothes in the cupboards, and the bed, and above all, having to endure people's sympathy. In a sudden burst of decisiveness and remarkable originality, I paid for my coffee and went and bought myself a ticket for a night flight to Paris.

3

I WENT to sleep almost as soon as we were airborne from Chicago and had to be awakened to put my seat-belt on as we went in to land at Orly. With the difference in time, it was still only one o'clock in the morning, and by the time I got to the Hotel St. Jacques it was after two. I was wide awake now, and there was no point in going to bed, so I simply dumped my baggage with the night-porter and went out again and took a cab to a night-club in the Boulevard Raspail. On the way I recalled how often, when Sarah and I had been in Paris, we had promised ourselves a night on the town, and how regularly, after dinner, we had found ourselves too tired and too over-fed to want to go on. It was different this time.

It was different too, when I got to the Villa Rosa. The manager was the same small fair man of indefinite age that he has been to my knowledge for twenty-five years. The room was as long and narrow and hot and smoky as it has always been. The act that was going on when I arrived—that act in which two of the girls are a bull and somebody from the audience, three-parts drunk, is invited to act as matador—was one that I must have seen at least half-a-dozen times. Even the girls at the bar, if they were not the same girls as last time, were the same for all practical purposes. Nevertheless there was a difference, and I realized that since I married Sarah, twelve years ago, I had never been to a night-club alone. Everybody else realized it quickly enough, and in five minutes I had two of them at my table, drinking soi-disant champagne, explaining to me that they were good girls, and game for anything, and inviting me to put my hand up their skirts and see what good girls they were.

I don't drink night-club champagne. I did my best with a couple of brandies and sodas, but it was no good, and by the time the man came in who falls flat on his face carrying a pile of plates, I had decided that the Villa Rosa was no place for me, and that all the forbidden delights which I was being offered in whispers were not what I wanted just at the moment. I over-paid everybody and went back to the Hotel St. Jacques and slept until two o'clock the following day.

§

It was fine to sleep until two o'clock, but even so there was still a lot of the day to be got through. And after that there would be to-morrow and the next day and so on and on. But it was lovely day and I went and sat outside a café in the Champs Elysées and looked at it all, and decided, coldly and without interest, that it was very beautiful indeed. Then I started to think round and round in circles again, and to do that sum which always came out to zero. I tried very hard to make myself want to do something—to go to the Louvre, or go down the river on a boat, or go to the races, or book a seat for the opera. But it was no good. I just went on sitting there, knowing something of what it would be like to suffer from complete paralysis. It was a tremendous relief when, after about two hours, I remembered that I had no tooth-paste, and must buy some before I went back to the hotel. Nothing else seemed to matter, but lack of toothpaste was serious, and I had positively got up to go and buy

26

some when a voice behind me cried, almost with ecstasy, '*Jim!*'

Roy Featherstone was a little sandy-haired man with a little sandy beard who lived in Paris in a very expensive apartment near the Etoile. I had known him for years, but I knew very little about him really, except that he was rich, a pansy, and given from time to time to backing 'advanced' plays. Roy was by no means my favourite man, but I suddenly realized that I was uncommonly glad to see him.

We shook hands and he pressed my hand so hard and gazed at me with such emotion and affection that I thought for one second that he must know about Sarah. But it was only for a second. How could he know? Her name had appeared in the Press in the list of those killed in the crash, but it had only been as 'Mrs. S. Peterson', with Petersen spelt with an 'o' instead of an 'e'. The point, of course, was that Roy always did press your hand and gaze at you with deep emotion. What was more, he certainly wouldn't ask after Sarah. Roy hated his friends to have wives.

We sat down and he said, 'Well, well, well—this is *quite* delightful. And what are you doing in Paris, my dear? Working on a picture?'

I said, 'No. I only got back from Hollywood last night.'

'And now you're relaxing and breathing in civilization again, after that *horrible barbarous* place?'

'That's right.'

'Well, you couldn't have come at a more splendid moment, my dear. I have a little party this evening, and it is absolutely my *command* that you should come. The most shatteringly dull collection, my dear. Practically every bore in Paris.'

He laid his hand on mine and gazed at me entreatingly: 'You'll do this for me, Jim? You'll come and be at least *one* person that I really want to see?'

I knew about those little parties of Roy's. I could imagine him laying his hand on the hand of various other people and gazing at them entreatingly and saying, 'But the most *ghastly* collection, my dear. Men from Hollywood. *Scriptwriters* and people like that. You must come and save me.' But I knew it would only take a very few minutes to buy the toothpaste and after that . . . ?

I said, 'That's very kind of you, Roy. You still have the same apartment?'

'Absolutely, my dear. Absolutely the same one. Six-thirty.'

§

It was only four o'clock, but the prospect of having something to do at six-thirty, even if it was to go to one of Roy Featherstone's parties, somehow got rid of the paralysis for the moment. I went and bought my toothpaste, and then took a taxi and went down to Notre Dame. It had been a ritual that whenever Sarah and I went to Paris, the first thing we should do was to go to Notre Dame and burn a candle to Our Lady of Paris. I bought Our Lady the longest candle they had in stock, and stuck it on the spike in front of her and lit it. Somehow the long candle looked rather ostentatious and vulgar beside the smaller ones that were already burning. It occurred to me that I ought to pray for Sarah's soul and I went and knelt down near the statue of Our Lady and tried to do so. It was not a successful effort. To pray properly needs practice, and I was out of practice; and anyhow Notre Dame, like most of the great cathedrals, has never struck me as a place where one is very close to God but only close to history. In Notre Dame, you are

28

near enough to Henri Quatre and Ravillac and even General de Gaulle, but God is not amongst those present. And so I never succeeded in praying for the repose of Sarah's soul, perhaps because I didn't really believe it could repose much anywhere. She was not a reposeful type. I just knelt there and watched the flame begin to eat, slowly but quite inexorably, into the wax of my long candle, and reflected that even the longest and most expensive candles don't last long. 'Put out the light and then . . . put out the light. . . .'

But if all this did nothing else for me, it took up a satisfactory amount of time, and almost before I knew it, it was a quarter past six and I could reasonably start in the direction of Roy Featherstone's party.

§

It was not only absolutely the same apartment, but absolutely the same party. I fancy that when I had been there last the big room had had black walls and scarlet furniture, whereas now it had scarlet walls and black furniture, but I may be wrong even about that. There must have been about a hundred and fifty people present, of whom perhaps ten were French. There was a man working a pneumatic drill on the road outside, so that everybody was talking even more loudly than they usually do at these affairs, and the place was reverberating to the sound of Englishmen and Americans speaking excruciating French. Featherstone dashed forward as I entered and practically embraced me, addressing me as 'Joe'. I don't think by that time he had the faintest idea who I was. Then somebody else arrived and he dashed off to greet them, and I accepted a glass of champagne from a waiter and took up a strong tactical position with my back, like Haig's, to the wall. 'Some of us,' wrote Haig in his famous message, 'are now very tired.'

I saw her almost as soon as I came into the room. The green frock was an unusual and eye-catching colour, particularly with that hair, which was the colour of old walnut. She was only about ten feet away, but she had her back to me, and I did no more than register general approval. Plenty of people in the room were wearing closely-fitting dresses, and in almost every other instance, this was a mistake. In hers it was not. I also noticed that she had positively beautiful, as opposed to negatively beautiful, legs, and guessed from this that she probably wasn't a Frenchwoman. But this was all, until she turned and I saw her face, and then for a moment the impact was so over-whelming that I heard myself give a curious sort of grunting gasp. She may have heard it, or I may have made some involuntary movement which caught her eye, because she turned farther and looked straight at me, and for just a fraction of a second it was all a bad dream, and there was Sarah, with me at Roy Featherstone's party. The same big eyes set in the same way in the same rather small face. The same high cheek-bones. The same habit of lifting the chin with the head slightly thrown back. The same arch of the eyebrows. The same definite curve of breast and hip which made her a woman and not a scraggy clothes-horse. The same long beautifully shaped legs.

It was only for a fraction of a second of course. Then one began to see the difference. She was slightly but perceptibly taller than Sarah. The big eyes had no green in them. They were pure grey. And in some curious way the ears were differently set. I had seen Sarah's hair practically every colour from blonde to black, but I had never seen it that curious walnut colour. But while I was working this out I was staring at her like a zombie.

She looked at me for perhaps three seconds, and then with a queer little movement of the mouth which was half a smile, half not, turned back to her group. It must be mildly embarrassing to find yourself being stared at by a zombie.

Roy suddenly came burrowing his way out of the crowd. He said, 'Well, Joe my dear, how are we doing?'

I said, 'Jim. Jim Petersen.'

'How right you are, my dear. Come and meet some people. Terrible people. Every bore in Paris, between ourselves.'

I said, 'I want to meet that girl over there—the one in the green dress.'

Roy looked round rather glassily and said, 'Green dress . . . Oh, yes. Can't keep away from bitches, can you, Joe dear? Green dress . . . ?' He passed his hand over his forehead and said, 'Now let's see—that's Lucille. No it isn't. . . . What the hell is her name? Anyhow it doesn't matter, you come and meet her, Joe my dear.' He took me by the arm and led me over to the group, pulled her away from it with an unceremonious yank and said, 'Lucille—I want you to meet Joe Prendergast—one of my oldest friends, Joe. Joe—this is Lucille. Bless you, my children,' and went away through the crowd with a curious burrowing motion which always suggested that he was on his hands and knees.

I said, 'My name, in fact, is Jim Petersen. Roy really isn't very good at introductions.'

She smiled slightly and said, 'No—he isn't. I'm Katherine Field. How do you do.'

I said, 'You live in Paris?'

'Yes,' she said briefly. 'Do you?'

'No. I'm just—on holiday.'

The illusion when one was close to her was less than when one was ten feet away, but even so it was still

31

remarkable, and the way in which she rather nervously changed her handbag from one hand to the other in the moment's silence that followed was pure Sarah.

I blurted out, 'I'm sorry I was staring at you in that very rude way a few minutes ago, but you are extraordinarily like my wife.'

She said, 'Your wife? Is she here to-night?' And glanced round the room with her chin raised in that curiously proud way I knew so well.

I said dully, 'No. She's dead. She was killed in an air crash a few days ago.' I don't know why I told her. I hadn't put it in *The Times*, or told anybody in England, or told Roy, or told anybody. But it came out for some reason.

She looked at me for a long moment, and I realized that the colour of her eyes was quite different from Sarah's. She looked away and said, 'I'm sorry.'

Something was slipping away and I wasn't doing it properly. I said, almost desperately, 'But you see what I mean . . .' and pulled Sarah's passport out of my pocket and opened it at the photograph. 'This is only a passport photograph but you'll see what I mean . . .'

She took the passport rather slowly and looked at it for what seemed to me a long time. Then she looked up and gave me a wry little smile and said, 'Yes—I can see that we're rather alike. Though I could never hope to be as beautiful as that,' and gave me the passport back.

As I put it in my pocket there was a tremendous yank on my arm and there was Roy. He was looking very glassy-eyed and he said, 'Come on, Joe—to work, to work! Come and meet the dullest man in Paris.'

It seemed to me that she made a tiny, involuntary gesture of protest. I shook my arm free for a moment and said, 'Yes . . . ?' Her lips opened but she did not say anything. I said, 'I'm at the St. Jacques . . .', and then

Roy was hauling at my arm again and cooing, 'Work—
work! Dullest man in Paris.' I was hauled away, and by
the time I could decently get back to her, she had disappeared.

§

One of the most famous things about the Hotel St.
Jacques was the old lady who worked the switchboard.
She must have been somewhere between seventy and
eighty, very deaf, and very short-tempered, and it was
possible to spend a quarter of an hour trying to get a
simple outgoing call. On incoming calls, her usual technique was to ring the first room that came into her head
and then to tell the caller that one was not available. To
leave a message was usually quite out of the question.
Yet either Miss Katherine Field must have worked uncommonly hard, or else there must have been a relief
telephonist at the switchboard, because when I got back
to the hotel at about eleven o'clock that night there was
a message to say that she had called me, and would be
glad if I would ring a Balzac number when I came in.

I don't think I was really surprised. I had felt, when
Roy pulled me away, that somehow there was another
bit to that conversation. But I had no idea what it was,
and so I went at once to my room and called the Balzac
number, to see if she had. The woman who answered
seemed a little vague about her, and it took them some
time to get her to the telephone, but when they did, she
said at once, 'Katherine Field . . . the one who's like your
wife. I want to come to see you.'

I said, 'Of course. When would you like to come? How
about luncheon to-morrow?'

'I'm afraid to-morrow isn't possible. It would have to
be to-night.'

33

I glanced at my watch. It was a quarter past eleven. I said, 'Well . . . of course. But it's a bit late, isn't it? I mean the bar's shut and so on. Everything in the St. Jacques closes down very early.'

'But you have somewhere where we could talk? I want to ask you something, Mr. Petersen.'

Somehow the 'Mr. Petersen' settled it. If it had been 'Jim' or even 'Joe' I think I should have politely refused. As it was, I said, 'Of course, by all means come along, if you don't mind its not being very grand. Two hundred and seven, second floor. I'll tell them to bring you up.'

She said, 'I'll be there in about twenty minutes,' and rang off.

I sat down and thought that one over. My main feeling was one of acute disappointment with Miss Katherine Field. I seem to have been in no doubt at all about the sort of thing she wanted, and I think I tried, without success, to visualize Sarah ringing up a complete stranger in his Paris hotel at quarter past eleven at night, and saying she wanted to come to see him. But there was nothing to be done with it now, so I rang up the desk and went through all the enormous complications of buying a bottle of champagne. In the Hotel St. Jacques at an unearthly hour like eleven-fifteen, it was about as easy as trying to do the same thing in a temperance hotel in Hull; but it came in the end, brought by the old humped-back man who works the lift at night. I strongly recommend anybody who still thinks that Paris is the gay city to try staying at the Hotel St. Jacques. There cannot be anywhere in the world which is at once as expensive, quite as dully respectable, and quite as badly serviced. I suppose that's why I've gone on staying there, whenever I can afford it, for twenty years—that and the comfort and beauty of those big rooms, with their delicately painted panelling and the furniture which could so easily

34

be genuine, and probably is. Even with the sleeping part of it discreetly curtained off, my room was still about thirty feet long. With that room and a bed behind the curtains and a bottle of champagne on the ice, I felt I was reasonably equipped to receive Miss Katherine Field, whatever it was that she wanted to ask me so urgently. Apparently she felt that because I had said that she was like Sarah, there was now some bond between us, and as I waited I wondered, with dull cynicism, whether that bond was supposed to involve me in lending her money, or taking her to bed, or only telling her how to become a film-star.

She turned up at about a quarter to twelve. She was still wearing the green cocktail dress, and though it was only a few hours since I had been talking to her at Roy's party, I noticed several things which had not struck me before. The resemblance to Sarah was still startling at first glance, not only in her face and body, but in the way she moved and carried herself. But she was younger than I had thought—I put her down at about twenty-eight, whereas Sarah had been thirty-three. The green dress was smart enough, but it had come from the Galleries LaFayette rather than Dior, and the fur shoulder-cape that I took from her, though sable, had definitely seen better days, and a lot of them. She gave me her hand with rather splendid formality, and as she walked across the room, I was vividly reminded of Sarah when she was shy, but bluffing it out—trying, as the Italians say, *di fare una bella figura*.

She apologized briefly for having come so late, and refused the champagne firmly and decisively. There was something about her whole manner which led me to decide, with relief, that whatever she wanted, it wasn't to go to bed. That left borrowing money or being a film-star. Yet when she sat down, she crossed those beautifully shaped long legs so that, in the short, tight green frock, she gave me a view of them to the top of her stockings, and when I lit a cigarette for her, she glanced up at me for a moment so that our eyes met, in the way that they teach girls to do in Hollywood, and as Sarah and I had done so many times as a family joke. I decided that wanting to be a film-star was the best bet, but I was still not sure, so I sat down, lit a cigarette, and said, 'Well now . . . ?'

She stared at me for a long moment with the big grey eyes that should have had a touch of green in them and hadn't and said, 'You naturally want to know why I have come to see you, Mr. Petersen?'

'Of course I am delighted, but . . .'

'You told me this evening that you were on holiday?'

'Yes. In a sort of way——'

'You also told me that I was very like your wife?'

'Yes. Strikingly.'

'And you have her passport?'

I began to see a faint gleam of light. I said, 'Yes.'

Miss Katherine Field knocked the ash off her cigarette and said, 'Then I want your help. I don't ask you it for nothing. In fact I will pay well for it. But I don't suppose a man like you is in need of money.'

It was on the tip of my tongue to say, 'Money is about the only thing in the world that I don't need at the moment,' but I decided that it was not a possible line and so I just smiled at her and said, 'We all always need money.'

'Good,' she said briskly. 'Because unless you wanted money too, I doubt if we could make a deal.'

All this was said with the greatest curtness and efficiency, whilst in the meantime the green skirt was gradually riding up until I could see her bare thighs above her stockings. I suddenly felt very old and weary

36

and said, 'Do you mind pulling your skirt down, Miss Field? You're taking my mind off the matter in hand.'

Her chin went up, and for a moment I thought she was going to be angry, as I hoped she would. Then she suddenly flushed slightly and muttered, 'Sorry,' like an embarrassed school-girl, and scrabbled at the inadequate skirt.

I seized my advantage and said, 'You've talked about a "deal". What sort of deal? What is it exactly that you want from me?'

There was a long pause. She looked away from me and I suddenly realized that her eyes were full of tears. I realized that I had knocked all the business-like efficiency out of her with the business about the skirt, and felt a beast. I said gently, 'Come on, my dear, what *is* all this about?'

There was another long silence and then she said in a low voice, 'I have to go to Yugoslavia.'

'Well, why not? I went there a couple of years ago. All you need is a visa.'

'That's right,' she said bitterly. 'All you need is a visa. . . .' She raised her head, looked straight at me and said, 'But you see they wouldn't give me a visa. And even if they did and I got into the country, the chances are they'd never let me out again.'

'Not on a British Passport?'

'I haven't got a British Passport. I haven't got a passport at all, because I haven't got a country. You see—I'm a Yugoslav. Or a Serb rather.'

I said, 'You surprise me. I guessed you weren't French, but I thought you were British. Your English is quite perfect.'

She said wearily, 'So's my French, and so's my Italian, and so's my German. English is my third best language. I'm not really anything. But I was born in Belgrade of

37

Yugoslav parents, and according to the government's way of looking at things I'm still Yugoslav, though I've never been in the country since the war. I call myself Katherine Field, but my real name is Katherina Feldic, and that's a name the Communists don't forget. My father died fighting them, just as my mother died fighting the Germans.'

I said, 'But that's all a long time ago. You can only have been a child when you left the country. Do you really think they'd still hold that against you? After all, I understand that things have changed a good deal in Yugoslavia since the end of the war.'

She sighed and said, 'You British never understand these things, because they've never happened to you. The Communists never forget, nor do we. I am Marko Feldic's daughter, and they're afraid of me because they know I hate them and always shall, for killing him and three of my cousins and most of my friends. . . .'

She said it quite quietly but with her chin up and her eyes slightly narrowed, and her mouth drawn down at the corners contemptuously, and I suddenly had a vision of Sarah talking to me about some entirely innocent people named Pearson, to whom she happened to have taken one of her violent dislikes. I remembered the extraordinary female capacity for hatred which has always puzzled me. But at least the Pearsons hadn't killed Sarah's father, or her uncles and her cousins and her aunts. I said, 'Well, if you don't like the way the country is run, and haven't been in it for years, why do you want to go there now?'

She hesitated for a moment and then, 'I have some business to do there.'

'What sort of business?'

'That's my affair.'

I said, 'It's all your affair, Miss Field—at least, it certainly isn't mine. But you came here asking me to help you, and I still don't know what you want me to do, or why.'

She took a deep breath and made a rather ineffectual grabble at her skirt and said, 'Very well. Then I want you to take me to Yugoslavia, travelling as your wife, and using her passport. It would only be for about a fortnight.'

'I thought it was probably something like that. And what do we do when we get there? Throw a bomb at Tito or something? Because . . .'

She sighed that sigh which I remembered so well—the sigh which means that one is being very dull in not grasping at once something which has never been explained. She said, 'There's no question of throwing bombs at anybody. It's simply a question of going and getting things which I am perfectly entitled to. . . .'

'Such as . . . ?'

'Mr. Petersen—my grandfather and grandmother are still alive. They are the only relatives I have left in Yugoslavia, and God knows why they're alive, except that they're too old now to matter. But my grandfather was a rich man before the war. He owned an awful lot of property in Belgrade and round it—big blocks of flats and so on. I am his only grandchild, and he wants me to have it, and to stop having to bang a typewriter eight hours a day to get a living, when all that is waiting there for me. . . .'

Her voice broke for a moment, and she looked away and swallowed hard and then said quietly, 'I remember when I was a child he used to take me for a drive in a carriage. And he would point and say, "This will all be yours some day." ' She raised her head and said almost with desperation, 'Don't you see that I've got to go and get it? Not only because I want it, which God knows I

39

do, but because unless I do, all that he tried to do for me will have been wasted.'

There was a long pause. I said, 'I think I can see that, but I don't see quite what you're going to do about it. After all, one can hardly go to Belgrade and put a block of flats in a suitcase and bring it away.'

She said impatiently, 'Oh, don't be silly. All that's gone long enough ago, of course.'

'The government has taken it away from him?'

'Oh, no,' she said bitterly. 'They haven't exactly taken it away from him. He's still allowed one room in a block that belonged to him, with forty flats in it. Of course he doesn't get any rent for the rest. But my grandfather was a very clever man with money. That was what he was mainly interested in. The law has kept changing, and every time the law changed he changed with it. There are some things you can always buy and sell, whatever the government says. He sold the vineyard that I used to play in for a single diamond. . . .' There was a long pause and then she said, 'That was my vineyard, so I want that diamond. It's as easy as that, Mr. Petersen.'

I said, 'So in effect what you want me to do is to take you to Yugoslavia, as my wife, and smuggle out such of your grandfather's assets as we can put in suitcases?'

'If you choose to put it that way—yes.'

'And why should I do that? It's all nothing to do with me.'

She gave a little shrug and said, 'I don't know. Money if you choose? There will be plenty for everybody if we do it. Or for justice if you will? Or just because we are *simpatico*. I don't really mind why you do it, as long as it is done and I don't have to type any more.'

'When you say "money", what sort of amount are you talking about? Five thousand dollars or five hundred thousand?'

'I don't know. They can't talk to me about these things openly in their letters. But in her last letter my grandmother said that the grapes in the vineyard were very good this year, and that I should try to come and help pick them, and that means that they're ready for me, and if I am going at all I must go now.'

I said rather feebly, 'I'd like to have a few hours to think it over.'

'Of course,' she said briskly. 'Englishmen always like to think things over, don't they?'

She rose and picked up her fur stole and said, 'You have my telephone number? The Balzac one? I shall be there after six-thirty. You can't ring me during the day because I am working, and there is a switchboard, and everybody knows everybody else's business.'

As I helped her on with her stole she said, 'This is very old now. I think it has the moth in it.'

I said, 'You're not speaking English as well as you did previously this evening, when you first came. I should have known then when you said that, that you weren't English.'

'Why?'

'Your grammar's too good. Almost any English woman would have said, "I think it's *got* the moth in it." "Got" is an awful word which English people use the whole time, and foreigners hardly ever do.'

She was standing close to me, and she smiled up at me and said, 'So if I'm going to be Mrs. Petersen, I have to learn to say "got"?'

This was a mistake.

I said, 'If you were going to be Mrs. Petersen, there would be a hell of a lot of things that you'd got to learn. Good night, Miss Field,' and opened the door.

After she had gone I saw the champagne sitting there in a bucket of melting ice, and realized that I should

41

have to pay for it anyhow, so I opened it, and poured myself a glass of it, and after that another. I had only drunk a couple of glasses of beer all day in the cafés, and one glass of champagne at Roy's. But after this second glass now I started to cry, which I had never done since I saw the wing dip. Because I wanted to tell Sarah what had happened, and ask her what she thought, and probably quarrel about it. I could imagine her scorn at the impudence of the whole suggestion, and her fury at the idea that any little Yugoslav bitch should use her passport, even if she no longer wanted it herself, and I decided that Miss Katherine Field, or Miss Katherina Feldic, could go and get her valuables by herself. It was all nothing to do with me, and I wanted no part in it, and so it was on that note that I went to bed.

* 4 *

YET the following morning it all looked slightly different. By the time I had sat outside the Café de la Paix for what seemed about a week, and had then found that it was only ten-thirty, I had begun to realize that something had to be done to get rid of this intolerable sense of paralysis, and my mind turned again to Miss Katherine Field and her proposition. It still seemed to me that the whole thing was really a wry Ruritanian comedy, with myself, apparently, in the Cary Grant part. But it was the only part that I was being offered at the moment, and at least it might be an advance on sitting outside cafés in Paris, and looking at my watch every ten minutes in the hope that it might be later than it was. I suddenly felt a gnawing envy of Miss Katherine Field. She might not be a very happy girl at the moment, but at least there was something that she passionately wanted to do, and which she was convinced would allow her to live happily ever after. But I had nothing that I wanted to do, passionately or otherwise. Even if I didn't eventually accept the Cary Grant part, I might as well at least read the script. She had told me not to ring her until six-thirty, and that left seven and a half hours to be disposed of. I have no idea how I disposed of them, but I know they were very long. I think I spent some time in deciding which restaurant in Paris was really suitable for a discussion on how to smuggle diamonds out of Yugoslavia,

43

and by six-thirty precisely I was calling her and asking her to dinner.

§

I think she must have slightly misunderstood the situation, and thought that I had been impressed by the talk of her potential wealth, because when she arrived she was a very different person from the rather pathetic refugee of the night before, with the big eyes full of tears, and hand scrabbling at the skirt of her frock. Her chin was up, and her eyelids were drooping with a slight arrogance, and from the outset she left me in no doubt that I was extraordinarily lucky to be allowed in on this fabulous operation. She was wearing a simple black frock, which to my male eye might have cost anything between fifteen pounds and five hundred, and almost certainly cost ten. She was also wearing a vast brass chain and a plaque, which I think must have come from the Balkans. It made her look rather like a female sommelier, and it clanked as she walked. We swept into Les Grands Vefours with splendid dignity, clanking loudly, and she at once objected to the table that I had booked, and bullied the head-waiter in exquisite French into finding us another. She then examined the menu, and laid it down with a sigh of boredom. Clearly, I was being informed, Miss Katherine Field had been used to better things, and coming to one of the best restaurants in the world was just a bore.

I enjoyed all this immensely. Sarah herself could not have put up a more glorious baby-snob-bluffing-it-out performance. I carefully avoided catching the waiter's eye, and settled down happily to my role as the humble hireling. If Miss Katherine Field could be persuaded to go on behaving like this, then the comic possibilities

44

were much greater than I had supposed. By gentle and obsequious pressure I managed to get her to order a large and vastly expensive meal, since I suspected that it was probably the first decent meal she had had for some time. I remembered that in our last few years together I had been in the habit of making Sarah choose the wine, because it was good practice for her in knowing what the whole wine affair is about. The sommelier came and said, 'Good evening, Mr. Petersen,' in his exquisite professor's English, and I said, 'Good evening, Monsieur le Sommelier,' and we shook hands.

I saw a shadow of irritation pass over Miss Katherine Field's face, and realized that I had done the wrong thing. One should not shake hands with the sommelier, even if one has known him for twenty years, and not seen him for two.

I said, 'Would you care to choose some wine, or shall we just tell Monsieur le Sommelier what we're eating, and leave it to him? That's what I usually do here?'

She took the wine-list without a word, looked at it for a few moments and then said curtly, 'I think number seventy-seven.'

The sommelier bowed and smiled approvingly. It was indeed an excellent though very expensive Burgundy and very suitable to what we were eating.

When the sommelier had gone I said, 'Do you like wine?'

'No,' she said briefly. 'I hardly ever drink it.'

'But you ordered an excellent Burgundy?'

'Why not? You'll probably like it and I wasn't brought up in a slum. What I *would* like is some San Pellegrino, if you can catch a waiter . . . Well—how about it?'

'How about what?'

'What we talked about last night?'

45

'Hadn't we better have dinner first, and talk afterwards?'

'All right,' she said wearily, 'I suppose so.'

She ate the whole lot of it—the *crevettes* Rothschild, the steak, and two portions of wild strawberry tart with mountains of cream, and the cheeses, and then started on the petits fours as though she was hungry. It must have been a full hour later that they brought the coffee, and I could say, 'Well now—about this proposition of yours. . . .'

'Well?'

She said it calmly—almost indifferently. But her eyes came up to mine, and I saw in them a flash of mingled hope and fear. Miss Field certainly wanted to be taken to Yugoslavia very much indeed.

I said, 'I feel rather inclined to do it—that is, if you can give me a few more details.'

Her eyes closed for just a second and I heard her take a sharp breath. Then she said, with that fine air of indifference, 'Of course. What do you want to know?'

'What exactly do you want to bring out? Diamonds and things like that?'

'I don't know exactly until I get there. There is a diamond that he took for the vineyard . . . and there is all my grandmother's jewellery. Then there is quite a lot of actual money.'

'In banknotes?'

'Good heavens no,' she said contemptuously, 'In gold, of course.'

'Gold's rather awkward stuff to carry—if there's much of it.'

'I don't know how much there is.'

I said, 'It's nothing to do with me, but if we go and get these things, what are your grandparents going to live on?'

She gave a little shrug and said, 'They will arrange that. They are very old now and there is nothing left for them. They live in one room and my grandfather is very sick. They don't care any more. I am their only grandchild, and they want me to have the money. That's all.'

She looked down at the table-cloth and said in a low voice, almost to herself, 'I have a right to it. He always promised me—my grandfather—that I should have money. . . .'

'And what do *I* have to do—apart from taking you there as my wife, and getting you out again?'

'You don't have to do anything. It will all be arranged.'

'And what do I get out of it, apart from a holiday and the pleasure of your company?'

'That is for you to say. It would only take about a fortnight.'

Just for fun I said, 'Well, what the Americans call my "going rate" is about three thousand dollars a week.'

She looked at me in silence for a moment. and then her chin went up and she said calmly, 'That would be six thousand dollars. Very well.'

'Plus expenses of course.'

'Naturally.'

It was beautifully casually done, and I was vividly reminded of Sarah going into a shop during one of our broke periods and casually pricing a fur coat which would have cost just over three thousand pounds. When told the price she had turned to me, and said, 'That doesn't seem to be bad at all, for what it is,' and I had solemnly agreed that it was not at all bad. I doubt if we had three thousand pence at the time, and I very much doubted now whether Miss Katherine Field had six thousand cents, let alone six thousand dollars.

I said, 'I think if you were going to travel as my wife, the only way would be for me to pay all the expenses—

fares, and hotels and so on, and then for us to settle up when we get back. After all, if you were to start paying for things, it might arouse suspicion.'

She looked at me sharply for a moment and then looked away and said thoughtfully, 'Yes . . . That might be the best way. It would be quite agreeable to me.'

I mentally placed this in my collection of magnificent understatements. Whatever else one might feel about Miss Katherine Field, she certainly kept her end up.

I was just about to say, 'Well, let's have a liqueur on the expense account,' when I saw Joe Leary.

He was standing just inside the door, looking even taller and lankier than usual, talking to the maitre d'hotel. He had a blonde girl with him, but whether it was the same blonde girl as last time, I had no idea. I turned my head away quickly and said quietly to Katherina, 'If you're going to be Sarah, I think there's a chance coming up for you to start now. The tall man standing in the doorway is Joe Leary. He's a publicity man in Rome. He'll almost certainly come over. You've met him a couple of times before, in Rome two years ago. Don't worry if he sounds as though you were childhood friends. Joe always sounds like that.'

At that moment there was a cry of, 'Well I'll be darned . . . !' and I turned my head to see Leary bearing down upon us with the blonde following.

Katherina said quickly, 'Is she his wife? Do I know her?'

I just had time to say, 'Not sure. I don't think so,' and then Leary was pumping my hand and saying:

'Well, of all things. Jim and the bride.'

He turned to the blonde and said, 'Honey, come and meet Jim and Sarah Petersen. This is Jennie. Let's see now—did you two meet Jennie when you came to the apartment?'

48

We all solemnly agreed that we didn't think so, and we were almost certainly right, because it was most improbable that Joe would have the same blonde about for two years, but we all shook hands and made the appropriate noises.

Joe said to the blonde, 'Honey, you'll have to know it sooner or later. This Sarah here is my favourite girl. The only trouble is that she's so struck on this guy Petersen. I can't see what she sees in him.'

He sat down uninvited beside Katherina and said with deep sympathy, 'Does he still beat you, honey? The way he used to? Or has he given that up?'

It struck me that Katherina probably had little experience of American publicity men and I was about to cut in when she gave him her delightful, rather urchinlike grin, opened the big eyes very wide and said, 'Oh, he still beats me of course. But only when I deserve it.'

Joe said, 'You couldn't deserve it. He's a brute. Why not face it and leave him? Say, why don't you two come over and join us?'

I said, 'We've just finished, Joe. We're on our way out. But have a drink with us before we go.'

They stayed through two large dry Martinis. On the whole Katherina did very well. I suppose any intelligent young woman could carry on that sort of conversation with Joe Leary almost indefinitely. But there were a couple of sticky moments. One was when he turned to Katherina and said, 'Did you ever buy that villa?'

I suddenly remembered that when we had seen him last, Sarah and I had been thinking of buying the villa near Rapallo, and must have told him about it. Katherina hesitated for a moment, and her eyes came up to mine. I gave her a quick shake of the head and she said, 'No. We didn't buy it.'

'Why ever not? You were all set on it.'

Katherina said calmly, 'You must ask Jim that. Personally I was all for it.'

As we came away from seeing the place, we had held hands in the car as we tried to work out whether we could possibly afford it, and Sarah said, '. . . but not if it means that you're going to have to work even harder.'

I suddenly hated Joe Leary and his blonde and Katherina Feldic and said dully, 'Well, just after that I went off to Japan and then to Hollywood, and what with one thing and another it didn't seem worth it.'

The blonde said to Katherina, 'So you never got your villa?'

Katherina said, 'No.'

And I added mentally, 'Never, never, never.'

The other sticky moment came just before we parted, when Joe, who had had a couple of large Martinis with us and, I suspect, quite a number on his own expense account before, suddenly turned to Katherina and said, 'And how are all those lovely kids of yours? Any of them with you?'

I gave her the quick shake of the head, but that might only mean that they weren't with us.

I said quickly, 'You're thinking of two other people, aren't you, Joe. We haven't got any kids.'

He said carefully, 'You're quite right, Jim, absolutely right. Thinking of Dan and Phyllis Martin. Got lots of kids. What is it, honey . . . six?'

It was half past ten before we could get them to go to their table to eat, and pay our bill and go.

As we walked down the street, Katherina said in a low voice, almost breathlessly, 'I don't think he believed it. I think he knew I wasn't your wife.'

I glanced at her and saw that she was looking pale and agitated. I said, 'Don't be silly. Of course he thought you were Sarah. He even remembered that your name *was* Sarah, which surprised me. After all you are very like her, and Joe had only met her a couple of times two years ago. Meeting you with me he would naturally think you were the same girl.'

'Then why did he try to trap me? That question about children . . .'

I said, 'He wasn't trying to trap you, my dear. He was just rather drunk, and mixing us up with another couple.'

'Then the woman—she knew. I could tell from the way she looked at me. A woman would remember another woman better than a man.'

'As far as I know she never even saw Sarah. She was just looking at your clothes. Anyhow, would it matter if an American publicity man who lives in Rome had spotted that you weren't Sarah?'

She said tensely, 'It would matter if anybody knew. *Anybody*. Where the Communists are concerned, you must not trust people.' She gave a little sigh and said wearily, 'You don't understand what it's really like.'

I said, 'Look Katherina, if you're going to see a Communist agent behind every tree, all of them bent on trapping you, this expedition is going to be rather a strain. It's just after ten o'clock. What would you like to do now?'

'There are some people I have to see—people who know a lot about Yugoslavia. I want you to meet them. They will tell you some things that you should know.'

'All right. Lead me to them.'

We picked up a cab at the bottom of the Avenue de l'Opera, and she gave an address which meant nothing to me, but we started off as though heading for the Left Bank. As we were crossing the Pont Neuf, Katherina said, 'The trouble is that I don't know enough about your wife. If I'm going to be in Yugoslavia with you and pretend that I am your Sarah, I must know everything about her. *Everything*, so that nobody can catch me out.'

'But surely in Yugoslavia there won't be any problem? Nobody there knew Sarah, and the only person I know myself is the chap who's Second Secretary at the Embassy in Belgrade.'

She shook her head, 'There you are, you see. You know somebody at the Embassy. We meet him. He sees that I am not Sarah, he mentions it to somebody else, and in a few hours it is back to Them. That is what Belgrade is like.'

I sighed and said, 'All right—have it your own way. What do you suggest we should do about it?'

'It will be several days before we can get our visas. During that time we should be seen together, all the while in Paris, and you should tell me all you can about her, so that I know the part that I am playing.'

I said slightly viciously, 'Well, I can start now. Sarah loved to dramatize things, and once she got a cockeyed idea in her head, nothing could shift it. You won't have any difficulty with those two bits anyway.'

The taxi slowed down and she said, 'Here we are.'

I had lost track of where we were, but from the time it took I should guess that the place was somewhere in the general area of Saint Germain. It was a back street, and it was a small restaurant. The only people in it were two men at the far end who were playing dominoes. They glanced up at us for a long moment as we entered, and then went back to their game. The proprietor came forward and greeted Katherina with a slight smile. They talked together in what I recognized as Serbo-Croat in low voices for a few moments, and then the proprietor showed us to a table and went away. I glanced at the menu and saw that it included cevapcici and several other dishes whose names I remembered from our holiday in Dubrovnik.

I said, 'We don't have to eat another meal, do we? I don't think I can.'

Katherina said, 'Oh, no, he's only gone to see whether they're ready for us.'

A boy who cannot have been more than fifteen came and silently poured us out two small glasses of slivovitz.

Katherina said, 'You've drunk this stuff before? Plum brandy?'

I said, 'Oh, yes—I rather like it—particularly the faint flavour of boot polish. Who are these people whom we're going to see?'

She hesitated. 'A sort of . . . committee. Or club. Something like that. They are all Yugoslavs who live in Paris, and they may be able to advise us. The chief is Popovic. He is blind now, but he was a leader of the Liberals before the war. He was a friend of my father. Then there is Keratov. He was a judge, and Simic, who was the editor of a newspaper. They are all very distinguished men. By the way, you don't speak Serbo-Croat, do you?'

'No. I usually recognize it when I hear it, and I know about three words. That's all.'

'Can you understand it when other people are speaking it?'

'Good heavens no. Why?'

'Well, most of these people speak English, but they'll probably want to talk to me in Serbo-Croat. I hope you won't be too bored. I'll translate for you when they say anything interesting.'

The proprietor reappeared at the other end of the room and beckoned to us. Katherina said, 'They're ready. Drink up your slivovitz and I'll lead the way.'

We went down the long narrow room past the men

playing dominoes and through a side door. It was a small room, and it had in it only one table, which might at a pinch have accommodated six. There were only three of them and there was no mistaking Popovic. He was a big, heavily built, handsome old man with a magnificent head of white hair and the sort of moustache that one associates with French generals of World War I. As we entered, he turned his head slightly towards the sound, but his eyes had the fixed, indefinite stare of a blind man. The other two were less impressive, and apart from the fact that one was tall and gaunt, with thick greying hair, and that the other was smaller, smiling and bald, I don't remember them in any detail. There was a bottle of slivovitz on the table and they all had glasses in front of them. Katherina went straight over and kissed Popovic. He took her hand and held it tightly and they murmured something to one another in Serbo-Croat. Katherina said, 'This is Mr. Petersen.'

The smiling bald man bowed and said, '*Enchanté*,' and the tall gaunt man said, 'Pleased to meet you, Mr. Petersen,' with a strong American accent.

We shook hands. Popovic said nothing, but just put out a hand which I took and shook, as he gazed past me with his sightless stare.

We sat down and the bald man produced glasses for us and filled them. There was a moment's pause and then Popovic said something in Serbo-Croat in his lovely deep voice, and Katherina answered, and they started to speak in Serbo-Croat. I guessed from the way the other two occasionally glanced at me that I was partly the subject of the conversation, but the tall man and the bald man took almost as little part in it as I did, and then only to put in a word deferentially to Popovic as he rumbled on in the double bass voice with the unchanging blind man's gaze.

54

This went on for what seemed a long time—long enough for the bald man to have refilled all our glasses twice—when Katherina suddenly said in English, 'Do you think you could say that in English—what you've just said to me? I want Mr. Petersen to hear it, because I don't think he quite believes it.'

'I say to Katherina,' said Popovic, 'that it is very important that no one should ever think she is not your wife. No matter who. No one. There is not anyone to be trusted or told. Otherwise . . .' He shrugged his heavy shoulders slightly.

I said, 'As a matter of interest, sir, what do you think would happen if the authorities *did* discover who Miss Feldic was?' The blind man continued to stare blankly at the wall opposite him, and the flowing white moustache lifted in a bitter little smile. Otherwise he made no reply.

There was a pause, and then he said, 'You should remember, Mr. Petersen, that a Police State is a Police State.' There was a little rumble of approval from the other two. I bowed my head to indicate that I would try to remember this profound truth.

Popovic said, 'As it is, even if they do not suspect you, everything you do and everywhere you go will be noted and reported.' His English was entirely fluent, but he had a marked accent.

I said, 'Because we are foreigners?'

'Partly, and partly because it is the way in which a Police State is run. One in ten is in the pay of the police, and there are plenty of others besides these. . . . Some of them the last people you would think. There is in Zagreb a Japanese scientist who is a police agent; and in Belgrade at least two Americans.'

I saw Katherina glance at me with a mild air of 'I told you so,' and knew that she was thinking of Joe Leary. I also looked at the big, blind old man with his splendid head, and the bald man, and the tall cadaverous man and remembered that none of them had been in Yugoslavia for at least twenty years, and wondered where they got their information.

Katherina said, 'Mr. Popovic thinks it would be best for us to go by train. Apparently that is better than going by air or by boat from Venice. They are less inquisitive on the train.'

The bald man said, 'Boat is the worst. Whatever you do, do not go by boat.'

The other two bowed their heads in solemn agreement. I said, 'All right. But it's a pity because I wanted to take a car.'

There was a moment's pause and then Popovic rumbled. 'A car?'

'Yes. I understand that it isn't very easy to get about in the country by public transport, so I was going to do what my wife and I did last time we went there—drive to Venice and then put a car on a boat so that we had it on the other side.'

There was a rather startled pause, and then the bald man touched Popovic on the arm and they conferred together in low voices in Serbo-Croat for a few moments. Then Popovic spoke to Katherina and she turned to me and said, 'They feel that you don't quite understand. In Yugoslavia nowadays very few people have cars unless they are Party members.'

I said, 'Then there must be an awful lot of Party members, because I remember nearly being murdered by the traffic half a dozen times round Dubrovnik. Anyhow, surely that's part of the point? We're *not* Yugoslavs. We're just foreign tourists. There were a dozen cars on the ship I went on last time.'

They thought that one over for a moment or two and

then Popovic bowed his head and said, 'Mr. Petersen may be right. It might be good to take a car. But in our experience it is best to go by train.'

The tall grey-haired man suddenly said, 'There are certain things which it would be best to take with you. You should take some soap and some coffee. There is no soap and no coffee in Yugoslavia.'

I remembered those long days on the terrace of the Excelsior in Dubrovnik with Sarah—the eternal coffee drinking, and watching her at the end of the day, soaping herself in a shower . . . I said, 'Is this a new development? There seemed to be plenty of coffee and lots of soap when I was there last.'

'Where were you, Mr. Petersen?'

'In Dubrovnik.'

The grey-haired man and the bald man looked at one another and both raised their hands in a helpless gesture. Popovic continued to gaze blankly in front of him. The grey-haired man said with sudden passion, 'Dubrovnik . . . ! You people go to Dubrovnik and you think you have seen Yugoslavia. Of course in Dubrovnik you have what you want to see, what they want you to see. But you have not seen the children dying in the streets of hunger in Belgrade—in Zagreb—in Sarajevo . . .'

I saw Popovic's head come up, so that his sightless eyes were staring higher up on the wall and realized for the first time what I was up against. I was talking about a country which I only knew from a few weeks' visit as a tourist, to an ex-leader of its Liberal Party, an ex-judge, and an ex-newspaper editor, all of whom had been sitting in Paris for twenty years. I realized that all this mattered to them and didn't matter to me, and I said humbly, 'You must forgive me—I really know nothing about the country at all. How could I, compared with you gentlemen?'

There was a silence after that, and during it the bald man poured out some more slivovitz in what seemed to me a hopeful way. Then Popovic suddenly lowered that great white head and put his hand over his sightless eyes and said dully, 'It is best in our experience, that you should go by train. The train is less closely inspected than a boat or an aeroplane.'

I looked at Katherina and said, 'Then by train be it. Perhaps we can pick up a car on the other side.'

The ex-editor said, 'It is particularly important to realize that the travel agency is controlled by the government and that any arrangement you make with it will at once be reported to the police. The same is true of the hotels.'

We went on like this for about two hours, and at the end of that time we seemed to have been advised that Yugoslavia was a country in which everybody who wasn't dying of starvation or lacked of the ordinary necessities of life was a member of the secret police or in their pay. Popovic tired visibly towards the end of the interview, and when we eventually took our leave and Katherina kissed him, I saw that his sightless eyes were full of tears.

As we drove away I said to Katherina, 'Now what do those people do? I mean what do they live on?'

She shrugged. 'Popovic of course cannot work. He has friends who look after him. They all help one another.'

'Yes, but somebody must have some money, or earn some?'

'There are some who manage to bring money out with them. I think Simic—the little man—still has some money. But Keratov, the grey-haired man, is very poor. I think he works on a stall on the flea-market.' Her voice broke slightly. She said, 'He was the youngest judge in Yugoslavia before the war. He was a great friend of my father.' She paused and then suddenly said fiercely, 'Why did you have to be so rude to them?'

'*Was* I rude to them?'

'Yes—very rude. You spoke constantly as though you didn't believe what they were telling you.'

I said, 'Well, frankly, my dear, I didn't.'

'How can you say that? You go to the country for a fortnight, and you argue with men who are Yugoslavs of great distinction.'

'I don't doubt that they were very distinguished indeed. But none of them has been near the country for twenty years, and a lot's happened in the meantime.'

'They're constantly in touch with those who get out of the country.'

'Exactly. And the people who get out of the country tell them exactly what they want to hear—which is that without *them* Yugoslavia is going to the dogs. Don't you understand that unless they feel that, they have nothing to live for?'

'Popovic is a great patriot.'

'I don't doubt it. He's a grand old boy. But you say he was a politician, and the hallmark of being a politician is that you think you can run the country better than it's being run now—particularly if you're old, and blind, and an exile. They sit there living by taking in one another's washing and drinking slivovitz and thinking about the past. Facing towards the west where they saw the sun go down, and waiting for it to rise again, but never looking over their shoulders to see if it might rise in the east.'

She hesitated for a long moment and then said carefully, 'I didn't realize that you were a Communist, Mr. Petersen.'

I said, 'I'm not a Communist. I'm not an anythingist. I'm just a chap who dislikes bunkum, whichever side talks it. A lot of that was bunkum and you know it. If you're not prepared to face that, let me take you home and let's forget the whole thing. Come to think of it, I shall have to take you home anyhow, because you'll need at least one suitcase.'

'What for?'

'Well, if you're going to be Sarah you would be staying with me at the St. Jacques. And since according to your friends practically every lamp-post is a Yugoslav police spy in disguise, the sooner we get together and are seen together the better. It's now twelve-thirty and the St. Jacques will be dead, but for the night-porter. I don't think he'd recognize Sarah anyhow, and you could have come off a night-plane, as I did. But the daytime head-porter, and the manager, and the barman all know Sarah pretty well.' It was probably the slivovitz, but I was feeling very masculine and decisive. I said, 'So there you are. What do you want to do? Forget the whole thing? Or go and get a bag now and have come in off the early morning plane? Or wait till to-morrow and arrive all proper and run the gauntlet of all of them?'

She thought for a moment and then said, 'I think I would like to go home now. I have to consider this and perhaps to pack my things. If I were to come to-morrow . . . ?'

I said, 'If you arrive at the St. Jacques by twelve tomorrow, I shall be there and you can be Sarah. Otherwise I shall assume it's all off. Tell the driver where you want to go, and I'll take him on to the St. Jacques.'

She leant forward and said something to the driver which I didn't catch, and we swung left and went across the river again. I remember that as the cab pulled up she said, 'If I am Sarah, do you ever kiss me?'

'Yes. But very rarely and certainly not tonight. I will see you at the St. Jacques at twelve o'clock tomorrow.'

I handed her out of the cab, and remember that she showed quite a lot of those unmistakable and beautiful legs as she got out. And then I was in bed in the St. Jacques and crying and despising myself for crying, and waiting desperately, like the Yugoslavs, for yesterday's sun to rise again. It was probably the slivovitz. Anyhow, at that moment I certainly hoped she would not come to mock me with that illusory likeness.

5

AND yet the following morning again it was all different,
and I was terrified at the prospect of going back to that
awful emptiness and negativeness that there had been
before I had met her. Katherina might be an illusion,
but an illusion is far better than nothing. I started almost
feverishly to work out some of the details of the whole
operation. I did not believe for a moment in all the
solemn warnings of Popovic and the others that we
should be surrounded by police agents, but nevertheless
there were a certain number of elementary precautions
to be taken. I had noticed, for example, that when we
were talking to Joe Leary, the blonde had been looking
Katherina up and down, and there were several things
that she might have found surprising. She might have
wondered why I let my wife wear cheap clothes and the
sommelier's chain, and more particularly why she was
not wearing a wedding-ring. I cursed myself for having
abandoned practically everything connected with Sarah
in Hollywood, and then realized that it would have been
unthinkable to use her things anyhow. All I had left of
her now was the passport and a couple of suitcases with
the initials S.P.

I got out the passport and looked at it. There was no
problem there. The vague particulars would do perfectly
well for Katherina, though the height was probably an
inch out. The photograph, on the whole, was a better
photograph of Katherina than it had been of Sarah. The

initialled suitcases would be useful. I jotted down a note 'Wedding-ring. Clothes?', and then suddenly realized the full Ruritanian comedy possibilities of the whole situation—the bedroom part of it. If Miss Katherina Feldic was going to be my wife for three weeks, and it was very important that she should behave as Sarah would have done, what on earth were we going to do about the sleeping arrangements? My room at the St. Jacques was a large double one. I don't think there are any single rooms at the St. Jacques. It was one that Sarah and I had occupied before, and I remembered that she disliked it because it had twin beds. ('I *loathe* twin beds.') I could of course book Katherina another room, and at the St. Jacques they would only be mildly surprised. But there was the whole question of sleepers on the train, and what we were going to do in Yugoslavia . . . ? 'If I am Sarah, do you ever kiss me?'

§

At exactly twelve o'clock they called me from the hall and the porter said, 'Madame Petersen is here, Monsieur.' I went down and she was standing in the hall with her chin very much up, and looking down her nose with half-closed eyes in the arrogant way that meant that she was extremely nervous. She was wearing her usual cheap smart clothes, and my first thought was that nobody who had ever really looked at Sarah would have mistaken them for one another. I kissed her and said, 'Hallo, honey. So you've made it? What sort of a flight did you have?'

She said, 'Quite all right. Rather dull.'

'Where's your stuff?'

She gestured towards the porter's desk and said, 'Here.'

It consisted of one large old-fashioned suitcase of

beautiful brown leather with the initials J. F. on it, and
two smaller ones which looked as though they were
made of cardboard and might disintegrate at any
moment. I said to the porter, 'Pierre, will you have
Madame Petersen's stuff sent up to one hundred and
twenty-two? Come on, honey—let's go and have a drink.'

As we walked through the long hall to the bar I said.
'Well, if you're going to be my wife we had better get
you some sensible suitcases with the right initials on.
I've got some upstairs.'

She said, 'I'm sorry but they are the only ones I have.
The leather case was my mother's.'

'Do you speak Italian?'

'Yes. Why?'

'Because the barman here is an Italian, and you usually
practise your Italian on him. His name is Vincenzo, and
he knows you fairly well.'

We went into the bar and Vincenzo came hobbling
out of the inner room. I said, 'Here we are, Vincenzo, the
Signora has arrived.'

Vincenzo said, 'Ah, Signora Petersen . . . !'

And she said quite perfectly, 'Vincenzo—*come sta?*'

I said, 'The Signora has just got in from America.
What I think we need is some champagne pick-me-ups.'

'Of course, Monsieur.'

While Vincenzo was getting the drinks I said, 'So you
want to go on with it?'

'Yes.'

'Then there are several things we've got to do. First
of all you've got to have a wedding-ring.'

She silently raised her left hand and I saw a perfectly
good wedding-ring of the old-fashioned broad kind. It
didn't even look particularly new. I said, 'Good girl.
Where did you get that?'

'It was my mother's. Only . . .' She gave a slightly

64

hysterical giggle, 'I had to think about which finger I put it on. Because in Yugoslavia we wear wedding-rings on our right hand, and I could not remember for a moment whether I was being Yugoslav or being English.'

Vincenzo came back with the drinks and addressed her in voluble Italian. He had always loved talking to Sarah. She seemed to keep her end up very well, and her Italian was perfect. Yet I saw Vincenzo's eyebrows go up once or twice and at the end of it he turned to me and said, 'Madame has been in Rome?'

I said, 'Yes. We were in Rome for several months.'

'I knew it,' said Vincenzo triumphantly. 'Always before when Madame has come here she has spoken pure Toscana. Now it is Rome—Rome. Always Madame would say "*ora*." Now it is "*adesso*." Rome—Rome. Nowadays it is all Rome.'

He hobbled away behind his bar. I said to Katherina, 'There you are, you see—you've put up a black there. You said "*adesso*" instead of "*ora*".' I said it purely jokingly, but she looked at me with the big grey eyes very wide and frightened and said, 'Do you think he suspects? After all, barmen . . .'

I said rather wearily, 'Of course he doesn't suspect anything. You are just Signora Petersen who talks to him in Italian. Where shall we lunch? The food here is impossible.'

§

Over luncheon we held a council of war. I said, 'There are quite a lot of things we've got to settle. Personally, I think you and your friends are making a lot of fuss about nothing, and that nobody we're likely to meet in Paris, and certainly nobody in Yugoslavia, is going to suspect that you aren't Sarah—or even care whether you are or not. But you all seem to feel that there is a police agent under every table.'

'You heard what Popovic said. It is essential to avoid the least suspicion. It is not enough for me just to be like Sarah. I must be just as she would have been, in every way. So that if we were to meet her own mother she would barely guess.'

'Well, we shan't meet her mother. At least I hope not. The old lady's been dead for years. But if you really think there's any point in it, there are several things which we shall have to do. Your clothes, for example.'

'What's the matter with my clothes?'

'Nothing. They're lovely clothes. But they are not the ones that Sarah would have been likely to wear.'

Her lips curled in a rather bitter little smile and she said quietly, 'Too cheap, eh?'

I realized that I was being tactless and said, 'I wouldn't have said exactly that, but . . .'

'Why not? Your wife probably had a good deal more to spend on her clothes than I have had. She could hardly have had less. Unfortunately, at the moment I have no money to go and buy more.'

I said, 'Well, I'm reasonably flush at present. So you'd better have some money and pay me back when we do our final account.'

She hesitated for a moment and then bowed her head and said gravely, 'That is very kind of you. I shall of course keep a full account of everything.'

'Then there's this business of rooms. I haven't booked you a separate room at the St. Jacques, but I can probably get one for you if you like.'

'Would Sarah have had another room?'

'No, of course not. She would have shared mine.'

'Then I must do what Sarah would have done. There are two beds?'

66

'Yes. The part you sleep in is curtained off.'

'There is a bathroom?'

'Oh, yes.'

Katherina shrugged and spread out her hands. 'Then where is the problem?' She gave the sudden little giggle again and said, 'Where I live now I share a room with three others. A woman and a man and a young boy. There are no curtains and the bathroom is on the next floor.'

I said, 'You're obviously an old campaigner. Anyhow that settles that. Then there is the question of getting our visas. I think that's quite easy nowadays if you have a British passport. At least, it was last time. And it only took a couple of days.'

There was a pause, and then she said in a low voice, 'I cannot go to their Embassy. They would recognize me at once.'

'They know you?'

'Of course, they know every Yugoslav in Paris.'

'Well, I don't think you have to go. I seem to remember that last time we just sent in the application form and probably our passports, and then I just dropped in and picked them up again when the visas were ready. Anyhow, we'll see.'

Katherina shifted rather restlessly and said, 'But there are so many things I don't know. I am to be Sarah. Very well—but what sort of person am I? Where do I come from? What . . .'

I said, 'Do you do shorthand?'

'Yes.'

'Then, this afternoon, get a pad and a pencil and I'll give you some notes about yourself, and you can swot them up afterwards.'

§

It was a lovely day, and we sat in the Bois de Boulogne whilst I dictated to her some notes on the subject which had always fascinated and puzzled me—exactly who Sarah was, and how she came to be like that. When taking rapid dictation, and concentrating hard, Katherina had a habit of putting a tiny bit of tongue out of the corner of her mouth. She also reacted to what I was saying, occasionally giving a little nod of satisfaction, or frowning if she was puzzled or displeased.

I said, 'Your name is Frances Sarah Petersen, but you are always referred to as Sarah, and Petersen is spelt "sen" not "son". You were born in nineteen hundred and thirty-two and your birthday is on the fifteenth of May. Your father was Sir George Rose. He was a very well-known surgeon and I think he was knighted for cutting some bit out of some member of the royal family.'

This got a little nod of satisfaction. Clearly it was acceptable to be the daughter of a knight, and particularly of a knight who cut pieces out of the royal family. But the nod was immediately followed by a slight frown. Katherina said, 'Am I Jewish?'

'No. Why should you be?'

'Rose. It is a Jewish name.'

'Well, you are not Jewish, but while we are on the subject, you're a bit of a snob, and if you happen to be nervous you are liable to show off and go rather comically grand. Don't worry about that bit—you do it beautifully already. I may say it drives me nearly crazy with irritation. I spend a lot of my time nearly crazy with irritation. The rest of the time I spend loving you very much.'

Katherina put that down and said, 'My father and mother—are they alive?'

'No. They're both dead. You didn't like them much anyway. One of the main reasons why you married me was to get away from them. You married me in nineteen fifty-two. You were a complete baby then, rather spoiled and very immature, but damned attractive. You've been getting more spoilt, more childish, and more attractive ever since.'

'So we have been married twelve years?'

'Yes.'

'We have no children?'

'No.'

'Whose choice was that?'

'It wasn't anybody's choice. It just happened. Anyhow it's just as well. You occasionally think that you'd like to have children, just as you think you'd like a pug dog. But I shudder to think what would have happened to them with you as their mother and me as their father.'

Katherina said, 'What is a pug dog?'

'A sort of miniature bull dog. They wheeze. Anyhow, for the first six years of our married life we lived in London, and most of the time in Knightsbridge, and then I started this awful film racket and for the last six years we haven't really lived anywhere much. We have just been moving from one place to another, dodging the tax man. In that time we have been in France, Italy, Beverly Hills, Mexico, Switzerland, and Spain.'

Katherina looked up with a slightly anxious frown and said, 'I only speak a very little Spanish.'

'You don't have to speak Spanish. You were only there for three months. As long as you speak French and Italian you'll be all right. But remember that the Italian for "now" is "*ora*" and not "*adesso*." Your Italian is Tuscan, not Roman. Not that it matters. None of this really matters. The only thing that matters is that you have a heart of gold—somewhere. And in a curious way,

69

for some curious reason, you love me. You are even proud of me really. But it's only when we are in bed that you let your hair down and tell me so.'

Katherina said, 'Let my . . . ?'

'Let your hair down.'

'Hair . . .'

Katherina uncrossed her legs and crossed them again the other way. She said, 'Are we rich?'

'Lord no. We have occasional bursts of thinking we are, when I have just done a film job. But we always find that we're wrong. You have about three hundred a year of your own that your father left you.'

Katherina frowned and said, 'Three hundred a year? But . . . ?'

'Three hundred a year of your own money. The rest that you spend you get from me.'

'How much do I spend on my clothes?'

'I have always wanted to know the answer to that question. Anyhow, I can tell you that it's more than you think. But never mind. You always look well dressed and sometimes positively exciting. Incidentally, you must go and get yourself some clothes to-morrow.'

'How much can I spend?'

'We're reasonably well off at the moment, so you can spend a thousand dollars. And not a penny more, mind you.'

'A thousand dollars is not much, if I'm to be well dressed.'

'Well, it's all you're going to get. Remember that you've got to pay it back later, so you'll really be spending your own money.'

'But I have three hundred pounds of my own as well?'

'No, you haven't. You've spent that at least twice already. A thousand dollars is the limit.'

Katherina sighed and lifted her eyebrows rather superciliously, 'Very well,' she said, 'I can spend a thousand dollars.' It was abundantly clear that I was being mean. The sigh and the lift of the eyebrows on this particular subject could not have been a more perfect reproduction of the original. Katherina said, 'Have I any jewellery?'

'Not much, and none of it very valuable. But some of it very nice. Antique stuff. But unfortunately I left it in Hollywood, so you haven't got any jewellery now.'

Katherina looked up with a frown and said, 'You left it in Hollywood?'

I closed my eyes and said, 'Yes. What did you want me to do with it? Sell it? Or give it to a lady friend? There wasn't anything that really mattered. You had all the things you really liked with you on the plane.'

I saw the wing dip and that frightful cart-wheeling moment, and the little boy with the freckles standing out on his pale face, bursting into tears. The sun had gone off the seat on which we were sitting, and I realized that I was getting cold.

Katherina said, 'Other things about me?'

I said, 'You are a good cook, when you can be bothered.'

'I am a very good cook.'

'And you are a good driver of fast, powerful cars. With anything that isn't fast and powerful, you are rather a menace.'

'I do not drive a car. I have never had the opportunity to learn.'

I said dully, 'That's all right. I'll teach you. After all, I taught you before. Are you interested in your figure? I mean in keeping slim?'

'It is necessary to watch one's weight.'

'All right. But don't talk to me about it before I've even had my morning coffee, otherwise I get irritable about it. Looking back, it sometimes seems to me that

71

the last twelve years of my life have been mainly governed by whether you weighed five pounds more or five pounds less. And I don't *care*, you see? How would you feel if a man started to natter at you as soon as you got up, because he weighed thirteen stone five instead of thirteen stone three?'

'It is less important for a man.'

'Why? You're married, and presumably the man you want to attract is me. If I don't mind your being two pounds heavier, why should you—unless you are still trying to keep your place in the marriage market, and think that men like skinny model girls.'

'You like fat women?'

'Of course I don't. I just like to be able to look at a woman and see that it *is* a woman and not a man.'

There was a long pause and then Katherina said with a sigh, 'Men are very difficult.' She raised her eyes and looked at me and said, 'But you love me?'

The eyes gere grey, without a trace of green in them, and we were in Bois de Boulogne and it was cold. I said, 'Of course I love you. Look at the record. I married you, I have put up with a lot of funny business, and a lot of childish nonsense. And . . .'

'Only you sound as though you hate me.'

'Hate you? I don't hate people. The only thing in the world I hate is hate. Sometimes, when you behave like a particularly unpleasant paragraph in the newspaper gossip column—a mixture of snobbery, and envy, and malice—I despise you. But then there are probably lots of times when you despise me.'

'So we quarrel quite a lot?'

'Oh, yes. In fact about once a month we decide that we'd better part. And then we go to bed and make it up.'

Katherina put that down with a little nod of comprehension. She said, 'But you don't beat me, like that man in the restaurant said?'

'Oh, yes I do, if you ask for it—if you slap my face or something like that. As long as you behave like a lady, I try to behave like a gentleman. But if you start behaving like a fishwife, I am liable to behave like a bargee. I don't really feel that all this has anything to do with our trip.'

'But it is all part of being Sarah. From what you say, it is not easy to be Sarah.'

'No,' I said curtly. 'It isn't. It never has been.'

Katherina hesitated and then said, 'Are you . . . faithful to me, or do you have mistresses?'

'I've been unfaithful to you twice in twelve years—both times when I was a long way away from you and very lonely. It wasn't any fun either time.'

'And I am faithful to you?'

'Yes—usually you're completely faithful to me. I've always been surprised about it—particularly when I go off and leave you for several months while I'm doing some film job. Only once, about three years ago, you suddenly went slightly off your head and started to have a roaring affair with a very rich young man in New York. It only lasted a week or two and it was really rather pathetic, because you were terribly guilty about the whole thing, and would keep confessing to me, so that I had a sort of blow by blow account of the whole thing.'

'Did you beat me for that?'

'Lord no. I was only afraid you might get hurt, because he was a pretty nasty piece of work. In the end I thought you'd had as much of it as was good for you, so I just took you away. You jibbed a bit at the time, but I think you were really very relieved. You see, you and I may not be the ideal blissfully married couple, but we do like one another far better than we like anybody else, which

73

is what really matters. Apart from that, we're quite different sorts of people. I hate rows, and would do almost anything to avoid them. A good row is the breath of life to you. I like almost everybody up to a point, in a rather cold, fish-like way, whereas you are liable to take passionately against perfectly innocent people who have never done you any harm, and just loathe their guts. Yet when you like somebody and set out to be kind to them, you're far kinder and more sensitive about them than I ever am about anybody. That's the real difference between us. You can never do anything by halves, and I do practically everything by halves. I think that's enough for to-day. It's getting cold. Let's go and have a drink. You hardly drink at all by the way, because you're usually fussing about what it might do to your figure. But if you do drink, you like Scotch on the rocks.'

Katherina said, 'Scotch on the rocks,' and put that down. As she closed her pad and got up she said pensively, 'I don't think I should really like to be Sarah. It sounds too difficult.'

'That's what she always felt.'

'And you don't love me enough to make it worth while.'

'She always felt that too.'

§

For some reason I disliked the idea of going back to the hotel, and at one o'clock in the morning we were still in the Villa Rosa. Katherina said, 'Don't we ever dance together?'

I said, 'We used to, but we don't now. Don't you remember that row we had about it in Venice? In that place where you dance on a marble floor? There weren't many people there, and I was just enjoying myself when

74

you suddenly told me that what I was doing was hopelessly out of date. "Ballroom dancing" you called it. Apparently what we ought to have been doing was to stand practically still in the middle of the floor and wriggle slightly, and when I said that I didn't think that was any fun, you were cross with me and we had a row. I don't think we have ever danced together since. But if you want my frank opinion, I don't think you dance half as well as you think you do. You go and stand still and wriggle with anybody you like. Personally I'm too old for that sort of thing.'

'Don't be ridiculous. You talk as though you were ninety. Let's just go and dance.'

As we went on to the floor I said, 'Now that is completely out of character. I have given you a perfectly good chance for a squabble and you haven't accepted it. You must remember that if you are going to be Sarah, you *never* lose the chance of a row. Now what on earth is this that we're supposed to be doing?'

Katherina made a curious waggling motion with her hips and shrugged her shoulders up and down and said, 'It's called the push-and-pull.'

I waggled my arthritic hips as best I could and shrugged my shoulders and said, 'Well, it seems fairly straightforward. But if you'd . . . smiled . . . at . . . me . . . like that . . . in Venice, everything . . . might have been . . . quite different.'

At two-thirty the man with the pile of plates came in and fell flat on his face. We all began the game of throwing the crockery off our table on to the floor. I said, 'I've been coming here for twenty years and always he falls down with the crockery. That must mean that he's done it about seven thousand two hundred times during those years. It's a solemn thought.'

Katherina said, 'This is really a place for tourists.'

75

'Of course it's a place for tourists. I *am* a tourist. We're all tourists really, and a very short tour it is. Have a drink?'

Katherina hesitated and then said, 'I don't think I will, thanks. I put on two pounds last week.'

'To hell with the two pounds. Have a drink.'

'All right then,' she said carefully, 'I'll have a Scotch on the rocks.'

§

It was after three when we got back to the St. Jacques, and we had some difficulty in waking up the night-porter, who was sleeping peacefully at his desk. But we were very much awake by then, and judging from the regal way that Katherina swept into the bedroom, I knew that she was nervous. She might be used to sleeping four in a room with no curtains, but this was slightly different. However, she took off the vintage sable cape and hung it up in the wardrobe with fine casualness. I said, 'Now what? Bed?'

'Entirely as you like,' she said off-handedly.

'I suppose we'd better. It's fairly late.'

'Very well. Is that the bathroom through there?'

'Yes.'

She raised her chin if possible even higher, and picking up her more battered suitcase, which she had never unpacked, swept towards the bathroom door. As she did so, the string that was holding it together broke, and she had to make a quick grab to prevent its contents from falling out. She went very red, and for one awful moment I thought she was going to cry. But she recovered herself, and as I went across to open the bathroom door for her she said, 'Thank you,' gravely and politely, and went into the bathroom with as much dignity as anybody

76

could who was carrying a suitcase which had broken open.

When she had disappeared, I pulled back the curtains that cut off the bedroom end of the room and put on the bedside lights. It was a room that we had occupied before, and I remembered Sarah sitting up in bed one morning and saying profoundly, 'You know, in my opinion, Paris isn't what it was when I was young. But then I suppose it never was.' That exactly expressed my feelings now.

Katherina was a long time in the bathroom, and her re-entrance was rather striking. She was wearing a sort of imitation Japanese kimono in a rather unpleasant shade of green, over what appeared to be pink flannelette pyjamas, of the kind that I believe girls wear at school. The general effect was to make her look about fifteen. This fifteen-year-old effect was enhanced by the fact that she came in very slowly and casually, pausing in the doorway to switch off the light in the bathroom and with a slightly supercilious and bored expression, which was obviously intended to make it quite clear that she was feeling very calm indeed.

I said, 'Have you any choice of beds?'

She gave a little shrug and said, 'Well, have I? You're the person who should know.'

'I think you would probably choose the one on the left.'

'Very well,' she said serenely.

I added rather meanly, 'You hate twin beds anyway.'

She nodded and said, 'Ah—I hate twin beds. I must remember that. There are so many things to remember.'

I went into the bathroom and had a bath—one of those immensely large, immensely deep baths which are one of the few points in favour of the St. Jacques. When I came out she was asleep, and I think it was genuine, because her mouth was slightly open, and she had that curious

77

look, at once self-contained and utterly defenceless, which only a sleeping person has. I put off the bedside lights and drew the curtains, and got quietly into bed, and lay for a long time staring into the darkness and remembering more than it is good to remember. Four o'clock and five o'clock struck, but in the end I must have gone to sleep. The fact that in the end one must go to sleep is the only really convincing evidence I know for the existence of God. Nobody but the Supreme Genius would have thought of it.

★ 6 ★

USUALLY I am scornful of the people in books who wake up in odd circumstances and spend a few moments murmuring, 'Where am I?', and generally trying to get their bearings. Admittedly, I once woke up in an aeroplane over the Pacific and thought for a moment that I was in a London bus, but normally I am either completely asleep, or completely awake. On this occasion, perhaps because I went to sleep so late, I had a vague, half-waking period in which I realized that I was in the St. Jacques in Paris, and was quite sure that the figure in the other bed was Sarah, but went to sleep again before I could work out how or why we were there. But the next time I woke up, the sun was streaming through the curtains and the other bed was empty, and as soon as I saw the empty bed, I remembered.

Katherina was sitting in the other part of the room with a used-up looking breakfast tray before her. She appeared to have been studying her shorthand notes. She looked up and smiled brightly and said, 'Good morning. You had a good long sleep.'

I said, 'Not so very long. I didn't go to sleep until about six o'clock. What time is it anyhow?'

'About half past eleven. Would you like some breakfast?'

'No, thank you. This isn't one of my breakfast mornings. In half an hour I shall have a glass of champagne. Until then, what's the hurry?'

'You have to go to see about our visas. Often it takes a long time to get them. And in the meantime I want to go shopping. You said yesterday that I needed some more clothes, and I have no money. You were going to lend me some.'

I was feeling vague and heavy headed. I said, 'That's right. It was to be a thousand dollars, wasn't it? All right —we'll fix that, and then you can go shopping.'

'And in the meantime you must go to the Yugoslav Embassy and arrange about our visas.'

I said, 'Must—must—must . . . it was her favourite word. Make a note of it. Sarah had a passion for the categorical imperative.'

'What *is* categorical imperative?'

'*Must*. We *must* ask the Joneses to dinner. We *must* go and see a play that's been well revued. We *must* give up this house . . . and so on.'

Katherina smiled brightly and said, 'You're in a bad temper this morning.'

I said, 'I'm always in a bad temper until I've shaved.'

'Am I usually in a bad temper in the morning too?'

'No. Your bad patch is from five o'clock to about seven —particularly when you are just going to have your period. Then you'd quarrel with your own shadow.'

Katherina nodded and put that down. I said, 'See you in about ten minutes,' and went into the bathroom.

We went to the bank, and I gave her the thousand dollars and she insisted on giving me a receipt for it. We then parted, Katherina to go and shop and myself to go to the Yugoslav Embassy about our visas. She said, 'I probably shan't actually *buy* anything to-day. I shall just look around.'

I reflected cynically on the chances that Sarah, or anyone even remotely like her, would walk round Paris for a day with a thousand dollars to spend on clothes without buying anything, and silently bet myself half-a-crown that by six o'clock, when we had agreed to meet, she would have got rid of every cent of it.

The terrible Embassy, in which Katherina dared not set foot, was like any other Embassy, except that it was slightly politer and more efficient than most. The visas, I gathered, would only take a couple of days. After that I wandered down to the Champs Elysées, lunched outside in the sunshine at Fouquets, and considered the situation. There was no doubt that Miss Katherina Feldic was rather an ass in many ways, and that the whole idea of going on this expedition with her was pretty silly. But there was equally no doubt that she was a very attractive ass, and that she had plenty of guts when she had set her mind to something, which was one of the things I had liked about Sarah. But the main point about Katherina was that she was necessary. I had only to glance at my watch to be sure of that. I had lunched late, and it was still only just after three o'clock. There were still three hours to kill before I met her. But without her it would have been nine or twelve hours. I remembered that feeling of cold emptiness and shied away from it hurriedly. 'Women are not much,' said the American cynic, 'But they are the best other sex we have.' Katherina might not be much, but she was infinitely better than nothing. I paid my bill fairly briskly, and went and looked at cars. Despite Popovic and his friends, I had an idea that a car was going to be a necessary part of this operation.

§

I lost my half-crown bet. Katherina arrived at the St. Jacques at a quarter to seven, carrying two hat boxes and a couple of paper shopping bags, and bubbling over

81

with excitement. But she had not spent a thousand dollars. She had only spent just over nine hundred, and with that she had, according to her own account, bought half the town. Most of it, of course, would arrive the following day, and she presented me with a complete account, showing just what she had bought, where she had bought it, and for how much. The main items were a marvellous suit which had only cost two hundred dollars, and an even more marvellous coat which, by sheer genius, she had bought for a hundred and fifty dollars, when its proper price should have been three hundred. This technique of the detailed accounts was pure Sarah. As long as you can produce a complete account of what you have spent, including when necessary a sixpenny bus fare, the fact that you have spent too *much* money is somehow beside the point. Moreover she had been extremely impressed by the discounts she had been able to get when shopping in dollars, which was pure Sarah again. They both seemed to have felt that if you could get twenty per cent discounts, you only had to spend enough money to make a fortune. But I hadn't the heart to point out to Katherina that all this had happened to me many times before. She was too excited and happy. So I sat there and listened patiently while she explained to me just how beautiful all the things were, and how clever and economical she had been in buying them. As she sat there explaining to me just how the coat was cut and how fantastically lucky it should be that it exactly fitted her, the illusion of happiness was almost perfect. What more can you buy for a thousand dollars? I said, 'You seem to have been a very clever girl. You'll have to model all these things for me when you get them.'

I must have said it in the wrong way, because suddenly the animation died out of her face and she said formally and almost coldly, 'I am sorry. I am boring you. It was good of you to lend me the money. I shall of course repay it as soon as I can.'

I said feebly, 'I'm not bored at all.'

'You should have come with me. What is the use of buying clothes unless you are buying them for somebody else to like? Did you go with her when she bought her clothes?'

'Sometimes. But not if I could possibly avoid it.'

Katherina sighed and said, 'It must have been difficult for any woman to be married to you.'

'I think that was unanimously agreed. But never mind about it now. Tell me what you are going to do with the other hundred dollars.'

§

We dined at a small place on the Left Bank just across from Notre Dame. Katherina ate with enthusiasm. There had been no item in her accounts for luncheon, and I doubt if she had had any. She was beginning to droop a little after the day's exertions and excitements, and I remembered that she had not gone to bed until half past two that morning. But it had to be raised sometime and so I said, 'You know I'm still not sure exactly what we're supposed to do when we get to Yugoslavia.'

Katherina sighed and said rather petulantly, 'You have asked me all this before.'

'Yes—and you haven't answered me much. We go and get these . . . valuables from your grandparents . . .?'

'Yes.'

'And bring them out with us? And that's all there is to it?'

She raised the big grey eyes to mine, and hesitated for a moment, and I could have sworn that she was about

to say something significant. But she just dropped her
eyes again to the table-cloth, and started to play with
the crumbs of her roll and said, 'Yes.'

I said, 'Well, whatever your friends say, I think we
shall need a car.'

She shrugged and said, 'The car might be useful.'

'Then I'll tell you what we'll do. We'll go to Venice
by train, and pick up a car, and take a boat from Venice
to Rijeka and drive from there.'

'Popovic says that the boat is dangerous.'

'It might be for him, but it isn't for us . . . Sarah.'

I hated it the moment that I had said it but she didn't.
She said, 'That's the first time you have ever called me
that.'

I said roughly, 'It might easily be the last. But if we're
going to go into this business we'd better work it out a
bit. In two days' time we get our visas. We go by train
to Venice. We pick up a car in Venice. We go across to
Rijeka. We drive to Belgrade and stay in a hotel there?'

'Yes.'

'Then we pick up the stuff from your grandparents,
whatever it is, load it on to the car and get back across
the border somehow? That's the size of it, isn't it?'

She said, 'Yes—that's the size of it.' And raised the big
grey eyes to mine again and dropped them again.

'All right. Then leave the organization to me, and
stop worrying. I'll get you there and get you back.'

She suddenly said, 'I wish I hadn't let you give me
that thousand dollars,' and started to cry.

I said, 'Why not? Wasn't it fun shopping?'

'Of course it was. But . . .'

'Then why bother about it. Somebody's got some
pleasure out of the whole bloody muddle. Now come
home. You're tired.'

§

I can't remember much about our last two days in Paris except that Katherina went shopping for what she described as 'stockings and odd things like that' and that I went and got our visas without difficulty. Apart from that, and the recurrence of the flannelette pyjama scene at night, I mainly remember her coming to me after one of her shopping expeditions, looking very worried, to say that she had received a letter, and that it would be several days before we could do anything in Belgrade. I said, 'That's fine. It gives us a day or two in Venice. And who ever minded a day or two in Venice?'

After that it was pure nostalgia. Leaving the St. Jacques and paying their fantastically high bill, sweetened by everybody's good wishes, and taking the taxi to the Gare de Lyon to catch the Simplon Orient, which for me has always meant that one was going on holiday. Even the sleeping car attendant was a man I knew, and who pretended to know me. I said to Katherina, 'The lavatories on this train smell, and the sleepers were probably designed at the beginning of the century. But I would rather be on this than any Super Chief ever invented, because it is always going somewhere that I want to go.'

We ate the usual invariable French train meal—the hors d'oeuvres that come one at a time, and the veal and the crème caramel and the cheese and the fruit, and then went back to our sleeper. The bunks were made up, and we sat rather uncomfortably side by side on the lower one. I said, 'Upper or lower?'

'Upper.'

There was a moment's rather awkward pause, and then I said rather irritably, 'For God's sake stop this shy nonsense. Do you think I've never seen a girl undress

85

before? Take off your clothes and go to bed,' and turned away to that very complicated washbasin in the angle of the carriage.

When I turned back she was climbing neatly up the ladder to the upper berth in the flannelette pyjamas, and there she settled into the berth somewhere near the ceiling and said quietly, 'Good night, Jim,' and I replied 'Good night, Sarah.'

I don't know if she slept much that night, but I certainly didn't. There is a bit on that route where I fancy they put on two engines, when you are about to go through Switzerland, and after that there is a section where you are going downhill and you go really fast. It always feels as if you are going in great leaps, like some gigantic animal, touching the ground once in every hundred yards. Once, during one of those silent stops, when nothing happens but voices calling in the far distance, I said quietly, 'Are you all right up there?' but there was no reply, and when next I woke up and drew the blind aside we were obviously in Italy, because the houses were much too beautiful and much too badly kept for it to have been Switzerland. It was one of the oldest jokes between Sarah and me that you always knew by that when you had crossed the border, and it hit me, for the moment, with great force in the middle of the stomach. It was only for a moment, and then I recovered myself and called quietly, 'Wake up you there—we're in Italy.' But there was no reply and when I got out of my bunk I could see that there was nobody in the upper one, and it looked as though there hadn't been anybody in it for some time. But there was a bit of paper at the foot of my bed on which was scribbled. 'You sleep very well. Gone to have breakfast. K.' She was in the breakfast car speaking voluble Italian to the waiter, wearing the famous new suit and looking as fresh as a daisy. She had slept quite well, and eaten a hearty breakfast and now she was on top of her form and ready for anything. In fact, she was so bright and cheerful that I said, 'Take it easy, darling. If you look and sound as cheerful as this, people will think we're on our honeymoon.'

She said 'Well, in a sort of way we are, aren't we? Didn't you go to Venice for your honeymoon?'

'Yes. But that was a long time ago.'

'Never mind. We shall have two or three days there, and I want to do all the things you did on your honeymoon.'

'All of them?' I said coarsely, but she brushed it aside and said, 'I feel as though I'm on holiday. And I haven't had a holiday for six years.'

I said, 'How well do you know Venice?'

'Not at all. I've never been there.'

'That surprises me. But anyhow, it's fine, because if there's one thing I like it's showing Venice to people who've never seen it before.'

§

All the schedules of the Simplon had been revised and speeded up since I had been to Venice last. Coming as it did at the end of the journey, the long slog across the Lombardy Plains from Milan to Venice used always to be very tiring, but nowadays, by the time you have woken up and had breakfast there are only a few miles to go before you are in Venice. Nevertheless, after a while Katherina lost some of her animation and became rather silent and thoughtful. I could see that her mind had turned to what was going to happen after Venice, and to the awful perils that might beset her in Yugoslavia itself. She was still hearing the warning voices of Popovic and his friends explaining that the whole forces of the Yugoslav

State would be mobilized to catch her and shoot her out of hand.

To cheer matters up I said, 'We're just pulling into Verona, and if this is our honeymoon, I buy you a large peach here, and you eat it with newspapers wrapped all round you to catch the juice.'

The peach was a big success. It was enormous and very juicy, and she ate it giggling happily, while the juice showered down on the newspaper. She was further cheered when the sleeping-car attendant came in to give us back our passports. I took them both, but when the attendant had gone she said in a low voice, 'Let me have mine, please. I feel safer when I've got it.' I handed over Sarah's passport and she put it lovingly into her hand-bag. She said sombrely, 'You think I'm silly. But it's all very well for you English. You've never known what it is to be without any papers.'

We were just reaching Padua when the blow fell. I think I must have been dozing, when suddenly she gave a little gasp and got up quickly and pulled down the blinds over the windows of the compartment. I said sleepily, 'What are you up to?'

She turned, and I saw that she had gone very pale. She said breathlessly, 'That man—the one who's just gone by in the corridor. His name is Ferenic. He lives in Paris and knows me well. He is a Yugoslav who works for the Communists.' She slumped down in her seat and said helplessly, 'There you are—I told you, but you wouldn't believe me.'

I was rather irritated at being aroused from my doze. I said, '*What* did you tell me?'

'That they would follow me.'

'You mean that Mr. Ferenic is following you?'

'Of course. Otherwise, why is he on this train?'

'I can think of a good many other reasons why he

88

might be on the train, apart from you. After all, why shouldn't he be going to Venice for a holiday? Or to Belgrade on business? Anyhow, how do you know he's a Communist agent?'

'Every Yugoslav in Paris knows it.'

I said, 'It seems to me that every Yugoslav in Paris knows some remarkably funny things. Anyhow, he isn't much of an agent if you all know about him, is he?'

She was silent so I said, 'Has he told anybody that he's a Government agent?'

'Of course not.'

'Then why do you all know he is?'

She said, 'We all know instinctively. Nobody likes Ferenic, or trusts him.'

'And because you don't like him or trust him, he's a Communist agent?'

She made a helpless little gesture with her hands and said, 'I cannot explain these things to you, because whatever I or others tell you you don't believe.'

'Because what you describe as you and others tell me could be complete bunkum, based on the feeling that you're all far more important than you really are. Just because there is a man on the main express to Yugoslavia who you think might be a Government agent, you immediately assume that he's after you. Why should he be? Even if he is an agent, which is pure guesswork, there are probably twenty people on this train who would interest him more than you would.'

She leaned her head back and closed her eyes and said wearily, 'All right—all right. You know all about it. You know all about everything — Yugoslavia, and Communism, and everything. Now we shall see what we see.'

I said, 'Ah—here we are at Mestre. We stop here for a few minutes, and then we go across the bridge, as though the train was going out to sea, and then we're in Venice.'

She did not reply, but just went on sitting there with her eyes shut. Then suddenly she jumped up, pulled down her overnight bag, rummaged in it and produced a large pair of dark glasses, which she put on. I said, 'That's fine. Now all you want is a false beard and your best friends wouldn't know you. You look like a film-star in the old story—you know, the one who was looking round the cathedral in dark glasses, and somebody said, "She must be afraid that God would recognize her and ask for her autograph." '

Miss Field did not laugh or even smile. She just sat gazing out coldly through the dark glasses at the Mestre oil storage tanks, as though she thoroughly disliked them. Thereafter she was silent until we reached Venice, merely nodding briefly when I pointed out well-known land-marks as we approached the city. It was a sulk in the very best Sarah tradition.

The season was not yet in full swing, and not more than about a hundred people got off the train. As we stood outside the station waiting for our luggage to be brought out I said, 'Now, here's your chance. Everyone who got off the train has to wait while they bring the water bus up. Have a look at them and see if your pal what's-his-name's there.' She stared intently at the crowd milling around the landing platform and then gave a silent little shake of the head.

I said, 'No show?'

'I can't see him at the moment.'

'Then he can't have got off the train. He's probably going through to Yugoslavia. Anyhow, that ought to set your mind at rest. Come on, we'll be dogs and hire a motor launch.'

I told the driver of the launch to go straight down the Grand Canal, and not to take any of the short cuts, partly because I wanted to show her things on the way, but more particularly because I wanted to see whether it all still worked for me. In my heart of hearts I have never been absolutely sure that I really like Venice. Unlike, say, Florence or Siena, there is remarkably little in Venice which really shows the human spirit at its grandest, and most of what there is was stolen from somewhere else. For all its unique effectiveness in some ways, it still has about it a faint air of being a sort of stockbroker's paradise fallen into decay. Whenever I have not been to Venice for many years I have had the fear that this time the magic would have gone; and now, seeing it again without Sarah, I had been morally certain that it would be no good. But as we came up past the Ca'd'Oro to the Rialto bridge I knew that I had been wrong. Even the fish market, where Sarah had complained about having her bottom pinched, was a warm and happy memory. I pointed out the fish market to Katherina, amongst the other things, and she said sarcastically, 'The fish market? What a thrill!' Clearly the sulk was still on.

We had booked at the Europa, almost opposite Santa Maria Della Salute, and they had given us a fine big room looking out on the Grand Canal. Santa Maria was looking very splendid. I called Katherina to come and look at it, but she only looked for a moment and then turned silently back and opened one of her suitcases and began to take out her clothes. I said, 'Look—you're tired, aren't you, my dear?'

She hesitated and then said, 'A little.'

'Never mind—everybody always is tired when they get to Venice. Now, I'll tell you what we'll do—you have a bath and then rest for a bit, and I'll go and have a drink, and then in about an hour I'll come back and fetch you, and it will be just nice time to go out to luncheon.'

She gave an indifferent shrug and said, 'As you will.'

91

I went down and across the street to Ciro. It was almost startlingly unchanged, with the double doors that make it rather difficult to get in, and the bar, and the young man tapping out tunes on the piano in the inner room. Renzo greeted me by name, which was a pretty good effort of memory, and we shook hands warmly. He said, 'And Madame? She is with you?'

That was quite a question, and I hesitated for a moment. Then I said, 'Oh, yes, she's here,' because whatever else you could say, and in whatever form, Madame most emphatically *was* there.

It was the same in Harry's Bar, except that they didn't know me there, because Sarah and I seldom went there. But the place was full of Hemingway-style Americans, and I could have sworn that they were the same Americans who had been there when I had visited the place last. I didn't go through the arches into the Piazza San Marco, because somehow I didn't want to see it alone, so I went back to the hotel. I had only been away just over an hour, but Miss Katherina Feldic was sitting with her hands in her lap, fully dressed and ready, and her greeting was, 'You have been a long time.'

I said, 'Have you had a rest?'

And she said, 'No. I do not feel like rest at the moment.'

'All right,' I said, 'I'm sorry. Come on—let's go and eat. I think we'll go to the Colomba.'

It was a hopeless operation from the start. She was too tired to be hungry, and she simply ordered some spaghetti, ate two forkfuls of it and then left it and refused to eat anything else. She also refused Chianti or anything else to drink. After about half an hour of silent gloom I decided that something must be done about it and said, 'Well, come on now—why the sulk?'

'I am not sulking,' she said sulkily.

'All right—you're not sulking but you're not talking,

you're not eating or drinking, and you haven't smiled since we were in Verona. What's wrong?' She hesitated so I said, 'Don't worry—you're quite in character. This is just an ordinary Sarah sulk and I've had twelve years of those. But it's a rule of the game that when you've been allowed to sulk for two hours, and I ask you what it's all about, you must be prepared either to have a proper row about something, or snap out of it.'

She played with her fingers, not looking at me, and then said, 'I don't like being laughed at. Or sneered at.'

'You mean I laughed at you or sneered at you about Ferenic?'

'Yes. I'm not altogether a fool, you know.'

'Of course you're not. But you need help, as I do. As we all do. So what's the point of sulking and quarrelling when we need one another's help?' There was a long pause and then I said gently, 'Come on, Sarah. Take those glasses off, which you wouldn't be wearing anyway.'

She said in a low voice, 'I . . . I can't. I'm crying.'

'No you're not, because there's nothing to cry about. Take them off, and order yourself some food.'

There was a long pause and then she took the glasses off and blinked hard and said, 'All right. What should I have ordered?'

I said, 'Probably the *osso bucco*. You were very fond of *osso bucco*.'

I ordered it, and when it came she ate it ravenously.

I said, 'After this I shall take you home and to bed. Everything in Venice shuts down in the afternoon anyhow. Then, about six, when it's cooler we'll go to the square and listen to the band for an hour, and then we'll have dinner somewhere and keep an early night. Remember this is our honeymoon, and the whole point

93

about a honeymoon is that you mustn't try to do too much. Venice will still be here to-morrow.'

In the event it didn't work out like that. I had her in bed by four o'clock, but she announced that she wasn't sleepy and started to read, and went on reading until nearly six o'clock. Then she suddenly settled down and went to sleep, and was still sleeping with such concentration at ten that I hadn't the heart to wake her. I went out and ate a sandwich in the piazza and listened to the bands for an hour and then came back. But the note that I had left her was still unopened and she was still asleep, so I decided that this was the end of our first day in Venice.

I DID not sleep well that night, being haunted by the recollection of a time when I had stayed with Sarah in a room like this and we had seen a Venetian funeral coming down past Santa Maria Della Salute, with the black gondola carrying the coffin smothered in flowers, and the priest leading the rowers. Now in my half nightmare I saw this again, but this time it was Sarah's funeral, and somebody was asking me reproachfully why I was not going to it. All I could find to reply was, 'Cover the face. Mine eyes dazzle. She died young.' And then we were in the Colomba and Sarah was saying, 'What should I have ordered?' and I was saying, 'You are very fond of *osso bucco*, but it's too late now.' This happened two or three times with such vividness that at about three o'clock in the morning I had to sit up in bed and switch on my bedside light in order to get rid of it. I looked over at Katherina in the other bed, and she was sleeping peacefully, occasionally giving a faint snort that was like a heavy sigh. Somehow the sight of her there, undamaged, and peaceful and relaxed and very much alive, was poignant yet calming, and after I had watched her for a few minutes, I could stand the darkness again, and put out the light, and soon went to sleep.

I had been right. Venice was there the next day—very much so. It was a brilliantly sunny morning with just a touch of low-lying mist, so that from the other end of the piazza, San Marco seemed to be floating in the air.

As we went through the arches into the piazza, and Katherina got her first sight of it, I heard the sudden quick intake of breath beside me and knew, with something like triumph, that the place was on the way to making one more conquest. We sat outside Florian's in the sunshine drinking coffee, and as we were doing so the giant figures struck ten on the clock at the other end of the piazza, and the pigeons dutifully got up and volleyed round the square and sank down to rest again. In fact it was all very like a tourist's guide to Venice. I said, 'Now, let's have a plan. How long are we going to be here?'

Katherina said, 'I don't know. I'm expecting a letter to-day saying when they'll be ready for us. I shouldn't think it will be more than a couple of days.'

'That's all right. I've got to do something about getting a car, and you'll probably want to wander round the shops a bit. This is entirely a woman's town really. Apart from that we'll do a little gentle sight-seeing, and then in the evening perhaps we'll go dancing, or go over to the Lido and go to the Casino. Do you gamble?'

'I play poker. Is that right?'

'Oh, yes, you play poker. But do you play roulette?'

'I never have.'

'Then you'd better learn, because in fact you're a rather keen roulette player. The main difficulty as a rule is to get you to stop.'

'That's like me with poker. I could go on all night.'

'Well, you won't be able to go on all night on this trip, because we can't afford it. In the meantime, there's this business of the car. It's only just struck me that Venice is about the last town on earth in which to try to buy a car. We ought really to have got off the train in Milan and bought one there. But there's a garage here —a big one, just at the end of the road across the lagoon from the mainland. They may have something, though I doubt it. Anyhow, I'll see about that this afternoon. Can't you take those ridiculous glasses off now? I give you my word that there's not a Communist agent in sight.'

'I don't like having the sun in my eyes. Anyhow, everybody else is wearing them.'

'But when you've got them on, I can't see whether you're crying or not.'

She smiled and said, 'I'm not crying now.'

'Happy?'

'Very happy.' She put out her hand with a rather touching hesitancy and took mine and said, 'You don't realize it, but I really am very grateful. I know I was silly last night, but I was tired.'

I pressed the hand and said, 'That's all right. We're on our honeymoon, aren't we? Now, the first thing we must do is to go and see the Colleoni. It's a memorial that the Venetians put up to a famous mercenary commander they employed. It's something you must see, and anyhow it's rather difficult to find, and we'll show you a bit of Venice on the way.'

I remember that day as being the happiest we had spent so far together. Katherina seemed to have got over her fright about Ferenic, and once or twice she positively took off her dark glasses to look at something. Apart from that she was in her best mood, duly giving that little gasp when we first came in sight of the Colleoni, being impressed by the Doge's Palace, not liking the interior of San Marco as much as the outside of it, lusting for things in the shop windows, and generally behaving as though she was really on her honeymoon.

In the afternoon I left her to wander about and look in shop windows and went to the big garage. Rather to my surprise they had a number of cars in stock, including a very pretty little convertible Sprint Alfa, which was almost exactly like one I had had before when we were in Italy. I bought it at sight, and then plunged into all the interminable complications of buying a car in Italy and taking it to Yugoslavia. When I got back to the hotel Katherina was waiting for me, looking rather tense. She said, 'I have had a letter. They are ready for us in two days' time.'

I said, 'Well, that's all right. I've bought a car, but we shan't be able to have it for at least two days, even pulling every possible string and greasing a lot of people's palms. Anyhow, there isn't a boat till then, so it gives us just time for another couple of evenings in Venice.'

She was looking very pretty and rather pathetically worried and I very much wanted to comfort her. I went across and put my arm round her and kissed her gently on the cheek and said, 'Relax, my dear. Remember you're on your honeymoon.'

She smiled up at me gallantly and said, 'What shall we do this evening?'

'We shall go and have a drink at Ciro, and then another drink at Harry's Bar, and then we shall have dinner at the Taverna, and I shall show you the cat that sits at a table with you and eats shrimps one at a time with its paw. After that we shall go to Antico Pignoli and dance on the marble floor, and then on our way home you will ride a lion—one of those lions we saw this morning down by San Marco.'

Katherina said, 'That all sounds fun.'

§

In the event, it didn't start by being fun at all. In fact it started by being almost agonizingly painful. It was a

98

lunatic thing to do of course—to try to do a complete
reproduction of what had once been a perfect evening
—to try to put the clock back—to try to make the
illusion more complete than it could be. I think it was
the fact that Renzo in Ciro greeted her as 'Signora
Petersen' that really started it. But, whatever it was, by
the time we were leaving Harry's Bar, I had a real
physical ache over my heart, and felt that I might burst
into tears at any moment. Katherina did her best, and
chatted away brightly, but she saw that something was
wrong, and I think she knew what it was, because as we
came out of Harry's Bar she said quietly, 'Jim—you don't
have to take me out this evening unless you want to. If
you'd rather be by yourself, I shall quite understand.'

For a moment I desperately wanted to take her at her
word and to call off not only that evening, but the whole
silly expedition. But it was said so gently and sincerely
that I knew I couldn't do it, and if I couldn't do it the
only thing to do was to go full speed ahead and damn
the torpedoes. I took her arm and said, 'Don't be silly.
This is our honeymoon. Come on—let's go to the
Taverna and see the cat.'

After that my recollections of the evening get a little
muddled. I know we went to the Taverna and had
dinner, and that I drank a lot of wine, and that I was
disappointed to find that the shrimp-eating cat was no
longer in residence. I know also that we went and
danced on the marble floor, because I remember
Katherina saying to me, 'Isn't this where we have a row
about dancing?' and saying, 'No, no. That doesn't
happen for two years yet.' Then I was lecturing her with
owlish solemnity on the folly of drinking Italian champagne, and insisting on buying French champagne at a
vast price. After that the pain over my heart had gone,
and I was no longer worried about things like illusions

and realities. The moment was the only reality, and the rest was just ancient history. It was late at night and the Piazza San Marco was empty. We stood by the stone lions and I said, 'You just ride one of them, like you saw the kids doing this morning.'

She said, 'All right,' and climbed on to one of the lions. Her skirt pulled up and showed a lot of those very beautiful legs. She wriggled slightly and giggled.

'I said, 'What's the matter?'

She said, 'It's cold to sit on.'

'Aren't you wearing any knickers?'

'Of course I am, but they don't come far enough down to be much use.'

'Well, never mind—you'll soon warm him up. Go on —ride him cowboy. *Ride* him.'

She bumped up and down on the lion, giggling, and she looked so pretty doing it that I had to put my arm round her as she sat on the lion and kissed her hard for a long time. And as I kissed her I remember thinking that this had always been going to happen and was an inevitable part of the whole business. Then we were back in the hotel bedroom, and as I slipped into bed beside her I felt that she was cold, and shivering slightly. I held her tightly to me and she said, 'Jim—only one thing. Don't hate me for it to-morrow.'

I said, 'To hell with to-morrow.'

'Because I haven't done anything to make this happen. Honest I haven't.'

I said, 'What does it matter who did what? But I'll teach you to ride lions and be kind to me.' I pulled her to me and pressed her hard against me, and in that moment I realized for the first time that her breasts were slightly fuller than Sarah's and her thighs thinner. But apart from this it was the most natural thing in the world.

Considering how late we had been, and how much of this and that I had drunk, I woke at quite a respectable time the following morning, with no traces of a hangover. The only thing that puzzled me slightly was that I was in my own bed, and I had no recollections of leaving her. I went into the bathroom and had a shower and dressed, but when I came back she was still asleep, with the general air of a person who intends to go on sleeping for some time, so I scribbled a note saying, 'Gone to Florian's' and went out, and sat in the piazza and thought about it. I tried experimentally to see whether I had any of the proper feelings—remorse, or self-contempt, or the feeling of having betrayed Sarah or what have you. But none of it would really stick. In the end, all I was feeling was the sense of irritation at having done something which complicated things unnecessarily. I had drunk too much, and as a result I had allowed the illusion to become reality for a short period. To put it in plainer language, I had gone to bed with an attractive girl because she was like my wife. But how on earth was I to explain that that was what had happened, without being pompous or hurtful or both?

I was still thinking that one out when I saw her coming across the piazza to join me. She was not wearing the dark glasses, and there was something in her walk which made me reflect, with bitter cynicism, that there's nothing like bed to give them confidence. I got up and said, 'Hallo there,' and kissed her on the cheek and she said,

'Hallo,' and sat down and said, 'Do I look awful?'

'No—you look fine.'

'Well, it's more than I deserve. I ought to have big pouches under my eyes. I really am sorry, Jim.'

'What for?'

'Getting so drunk last night. I hate women who get drunk.'

This had a familiar ring and I said, 'All the best women hate women who get drunk. But I thought *I* was the person who got drunk.'

She said, 'Oh, no it wasn't. It was all that damn' champagne. Do you realize that the last thing I remember last night is dancing with you in that place with the marble floor? After that everything's a blank until I woke up this morning.'

She was looking at me with the big grey eyes, and it suddenly occurred to me that Miss Katherine Field might be a nicer and more intelligent person than I had assumed. I said, 'Don't you remember riding the lion?'

'Lion?' she said vaguely.

'Yes—one of those lions down there. You rode it.'

She gazed across the square and said, 'That's right. So I did. I remember it was cold on my bottom.'

'You said so.'

Katherina sighed and said, 'This seems to have been one of my more refined evenings. What happened after that? Did you have to put me to bed?'

I said, 'Oh, no. You managed perfectly well by yourself.'

She sighed again and said, 'Well, that's something anyhow. Never mind—I'm sorry, partner, and it shan't happen again.'

I suddenly felt a great gratitude to her and said, 'What —never again, Katherina?'

She said gently, 'No. Never again. People do such odd things when they're drunk, and then they don't like themselves the following morning. May I have some coffee?'

So that was that, all neatly and tactfully sewn up and forgotten, and we could go on from where we had been before—wherever that might be.

★ 8 ★

SHE had been very keen to go to the Casino, and it was that evening as we were dressing to go that she went over to the window and stood looking out on the Grand Canal. Suddenly she gave a little gasp and instinctively jumped back from the window and said, 'There he is!'

'Who? Ferenic?'

'Yes. On that water bus. Looking up at us.'

I went to the window. The water bus was just pulling slowly away from its station. A man in a trilby hat and a light overcoat was standing up forward. He was looking up at the hotel, and the lights from the windows lit his face for a few moments before the water bus slid away into the darkness. It was a pale face with a small dark moustache, and it had about it an expression of strange, wistful sadness. In the couple of seconds that I saw him clearly, I judged him to be a man in later middle age. He was quite small and stooped slightly, which made him look even smaller.

Katherina said in a low voice. 'You see? I told you— he's found us.'

'You're sure it's the same man? Lots of people look like that.'

'Of course it's the same man. I tell you I know Ferenic well. He used to come sometimes to the house where I lived in Paris. Nobody wanted him to come, because they were all afraid of him. But he used to come all the same. . . . He used to pretend to be a friend of the man who owned the house, but we all knew that he was really a spy.' She gave a little shudder and said desperately, 'What are we going to *do*?'

I said, 'What we're going to do is to go to the Casino and enjoy ourselves. What we're *not* going to do is to start panicking because you see a man in Venice whom you knew in Paris.'

'But he was waiting outside and looking up at us. . . .'

'He wasn't waiting outside. He was just travelling on a *vaporetto* which happens to stop outside this hotel.' I took her hand, which was cold and trembling, and said gently, 'Come on, darling—pull yourself together. Even if that was your friend Ferenic, and he's everything that you think he is, there's not the slightest reason to suppose that he's trailing you. And even if he were, what can he possibly do about it? You're Sarah Petersen, and you have a passport and a husband to prove it. Finish putting your face on, and let's go.'

The Casino was not as crowded as I have known it, but there were several roulette tables going, with people standing two deep around them. I said, 'I hate playing this game in a crowd. They're just going to open another table—over there where the croupier is counting the chips and getting them in order. Let's wait for that, and then we shall be able to sit down and play in peace. In the meantime you'd better realize that this is the silliest gambling game in the world, because, in the long run, you can't possibly win. You see there are thirty-six numbers on the wheel, and zero. So the chance of the ball falling into your number is thirty-seven to one against. Even if you get the right number you're only paid thirty-five to one. So in the end it's a stone cold certainty that the bank will win.'

Katherina said, 'Then why does anybody play?'

'I don't know. I've often wondered. Partly because

it's all rather pretty, with the cloth, and the wheel and the croupiers' rakes, and their voices calling the numbers. But mainly I think because it's only in the *long term* that the bank must win. In the short term—playing just for an evening—you may win quite a lot. And gamblers tend to remember the evening they won, and to forget the evening they lost as quickly as possible. Now you're the perfect roulette player, Sarah. You don't believe in statistics or anything like that. You just believe in luck. So you come here and you play some number or numbers which are the date, or your age, or the date of your birthday, or some number you dreamed last night, or the number of the taxi we came in. Anything will do, as long as it's a sort of divine revelation and nothing to do with anything as dull as a ball running round a bowl and falling into slots at random.'

Katherina said, 'It is the seventeenth to-morrow. It was my father's birthday. I shall play seventeen.'

I said, 'You have the idea exactly. The ball will certainly have been informed that it was your father's birthday to-morrow, and it will act accordingly. You back seventeen. But don't back it for too much at a time, because it may take the ball a few throws to get its instructions right.'

I bought some five hundred lire chips, and as we sat down at the table I reflected that the Lido Casino had a curious history as far as I was concerned. I have played roulette in a lot of places, and sometimes I have won, and more often I have lost. But the Lido Casino has always been absolutely consistent—I have never had a winning evening there, nor even felt I was going to win. Yet the people I have taken there have always won, as on the famous evening when Sarah got five consecutive numbers *en plein,* thereby winning ninety thousand lire, which she promptly disposed of the following morning by going and buying three handbags. If history repeated itself, I should certainly now lose and Katherina would equally certainly win.

History, of course, did repeat itself. Playing most circumspectly and economically, I never picked up a cent, whereas Katherina's seventeen came up twice in the first half-dozen throws. I could not help noticing the intense, almost fierce concentration with which she played, even though she was playing the same number every time, and that that number was merely something to do with her father's birthday. It was as though she was willing the ball to fall into the right slot, and that the ball realized and respected what was being asked of it. I had seen that face in its ferocious concentration before, and that hand coming out with its quick motion to grab the chips as they were pushed towards her. There is no gambler like your woman gambler.

After her second win in half a dozen throws I started to say, 'You realize the chances against that happening . . . ?'

But she just hissed, 'Be quiet!' and left her original stake on seventeen and pushed out another two thousand lire on to it. I was not in the least surprised when the croupier said quietly, '*Dix-sept,*' and the rake came down on number seventeen again. As they pushed the hundred thousand lire or so towards her and she picked the chips up with that curious clutching motion I said, 'It's an easy game this, isn't it—if you have the knack.'

She had a big pile of chips in front of her—perhaps a hundred and fifty thousand lire, as opposed to the ten thousand I had given her in the first place. As she gathered the chips in piles of ten thousand lire each, I noticed that her fingers were trembling. I said gently, 'Strictly speaking, this is the time to stop for a bit and see where you are.'

She turned to me with a curious, slightly glassy look in the grey eyes and said with a frown, 'Stop? *Now?* But I'm *winning.*'

I realized from the intensity with which she said it that to be winning—positively to be having some luck at last —was a new experience for Miss Katherina Feldic over a good many years, and a very important one to her, and that in suggesting that she should stop and count her winnings I had suddenly blundered in on some delicate spider's web of happiness. I said, 'Of course you're winning. You've won quite a lot. All right—you just go on and join me in the bar when you've had enough. Don't hurry.'

It was a table at which they spun very quickly. And at that moment the croupier called '*Quatre,*' and the rake came down on four.

Katherina said bitterly, 'There you are—I was going to back that, if you hadn't talked to me.'

As she had never backed anything but seventeen since we sat down to play, this seemed improbable. I recognized the mood only too well and said, 'All right—I'll see you in the bar later,' and went away.

It was about half an hour before she arrived looking cross and depressed. I naturally assumed she had lost the lot. As she sat down I said, 'Well—how did you do?'

She said with weary bitterness, 'Well, of course it was no good after you spoke to me. It broke my concentration.' She opened her handbag and took out two handfuls of chips and poured them out on the sofa between us and said, 'Here you are.'

I counted the chips and to my surprise she still had nearly a hundred and twenty thousand lire. I said, 'But you've done marvellously. After all, you only started with ten thousand lire. You've got nearly twelve times

107

that here. You'll be able to buy something really nice with this.'

She said in the same listless way, 'There was a time when I had two hundred thousand, but after you talked to me when I was playing, my luck went. Anyhow, it doesn't matter. It's all yours anyhow. I was playing with your money.'

'Don't be silly. You owe me ten thousand lire. Here you are—I'll take it. Now the other hundred and ten thousand lire is yours.'

'Mine?' she said bitterly. 'Nothing's mine. Not even twopence that I win gambling.'

I took ten thousand lire out of the pile of chips and carefully put the rest back in her lap and said, 'Well, that isn't twopence. That's about sixty-five pounds, which according to the way I reckon things belongs to you. If you want it, go and cash it. The cashier's desk is over there, across the hall. If you don't want it, just give it back to me, and let's go home and stop arguing about it.'

For a moment I thought that she was going to throw it back at me. Then she hesitated and said rather feebly, 'You do it for me.'

'No, I'm damned if I do. You're the winner, and you go and cash the money. I'll come with you, and after that we'll take a motor launch back to the hotel, and you shall pay for it. Is that all right?'

There was a moment's pause and then she turned to me with a sudden smile and said, 'All right—fair enough. And very much more than fair,' and got up and went firmly to the cashier's desk.

We were standing at the desk, and she was stuffing the wad of notes away in her handbag, before I saw that pale, sad face and the small black moustache bearing down on us. I said quickly, 'Don't turn your head,' but I was too late. Ferenic was close behind us and he said:

'Katherina . . . !' and instinctively she turned and looked at him. He came forward with outstretched hand, with a rather charming shy smile lighting the wan sad face, and said something to her in Serbo-Croat.

I must say that though caught by surprise, Katherina dealt with it very well. She half took the proffered hand, at the same time glancing at me as though for advice and explanation of what was happening. Ferenic spoke to her again in Serbo-Croat. She glanced at me again and then said, with just the right degree of hesitancy, 'I'm afraid I don't understand, Signore.'

Ferenic looked a little taken aback and spoke again volubly in Serbo-Croat, and I caught the name 'Katherina Feldic.' He was obviously asking her whether she was not Katherina. I felt it was time to weigh in so I said, 'Do you speak English?'

Ferenic made a little helpless gesture with his shoulders and his hands and smiled and said, 'Little.'

'Because I think you must be making a mistake. This lady is my wife—Sarah Petersen. I don't think she knows you, or understands what you are saying to her.' I am not sure that he really understood, but at that moment Katherina said quietly,

'*Vous parlez français peut-être?*'

'*Oui!*' he said eagerly, and launched into a flood of French. Surely she was Miss Katherina Feldic, and they had met many times at the house of Madame somebody or other?

Katherina shook her head and said, 'No. My name is Petersen, and this is my husband.'

Ferenic looked from one of us to the other slightly baffled, and then with a wave of a hand said, 'I see—you have got married recently, and so your name is no longer Feldic but Petersen.'

I could almost see Katherina whipping over the pages of her notebook, but she had done her homework very well. She said, 'No—I have been married twelve years, and before I was married my name was Sarah Rose. I don't know anybody named Katherina Feldic.'

I said in French to Katherina. 'I think this gentleman is confusing you with somebody else, darling.'

She gave a little shrug and said, 'Obviously.' She put her hand into her handbag and took out her treasured passport. She opened it at the page with the photograph and said, 'Here you are, you see—this is who I am.'

Ferenic looked at the photograph and then at her and then broke into profuse apologies. To his extreme regret he had mistaken Katherina for somebody he knew well in Paris. The likeness was extraordinary. A thousand pardons for having troubled us. We both said the appropriate things and parted with mutual expressions of regard.

As he went away I realized that Katherina's fingers and nails were white with the force of her grip on her handbag. She said in a low voice, 'We must get away from here. He didn't believe us. We must get away.'

I said, 'On the contrary, we shall now go and play. There is a seat, and you were playing seventeen.'

'But why—*why*? There he is now, standing and watching us. . . .'

I said, 'Relax. You are Sarah Petersen and you are at the Casino with your husband and somebody comes up and claims acquaintance, having mistaken you for somebody else whom he knows. The mistake is explained and he goes away. Not a very important incident, and certainly not one which would make you immediately rush away.'

She went and sat down slowly and hesitantly. I said,

'Go on—play your seventeen. Personally I have a fancy for twenty-three.'

I threw a chip on to the board and said, '*Vingt-trois.*'

She hesitated and then threw a chip on the table and said, '*Dix-sept.*'

I said, 'It's always best to let the croupier place your bet for you. Then there can be no dispute afterwards. Sometimes when there is a lot of money all over the table and people are backing a lot of different numbers, they squabble like cats and dogs about who backed what. Particularly women.'

We played for about half an hour, during which she just blindly put one chip on seventeen at each throw, and it won once. I still never picked up a sausage. Ferenic stood watching the play for about ten minutes, and then took a seat at *chemin de fer.* Across the big room I could see the sad, rather resigned face as he pulled the cards from the shoe. Katherina said in a low voice, 'Is he still watching?'

'No. He's playing chemmy.'

'Can't we go now?'

'Why? You're winning. Why not just go on playing with the bank's money and try to make some more?'

She passed her hand over her eyes and said, 'I want to get out of here. I'm tired.'

I said, 'All right. But let's go into the bar first.'

To get to the bar we had to go past Ferenic's table. I said, 'There he is—hard at it. Now we're going to watch *him* for a bit.' I took her by the arm and steered her so that we were standing well within his range of vision as we watched the game. He had the bank, and while we watched, it held three times. I said in Katherina's ear, 'Well, whatever else your pal is, he's lucky at cards.'

Ferenic had been concentrating with the peculiar concentration of the chemmy player, but suddenly he glanced up and saw us. He leant forward and gave us a little bow and the rather charming smile. I bowed and smiled back. He dealt the cards to a choleric-looking old man across the table, and then, as the old man called for a card, quietly turned up a nine and a knave. Except for the smile to us, his expression of quiet sadness never varied. I took Katherina by the arm and said, 'Now we're sure he's seen us, let's go to the bar.'

We went to the bar and I said, 'What would you like, Sarah?'

'I don't want anything.' she said listlessly.

I said, 'Concentrate, darling—concentrate. You've just had quite a handsome win. You would in these circumstances have a drink. What would it be?'

'A Scotch on the rocks,' she said dully.

'Correct,' I ordered the drinks and then said, 'Well, that was all very reassuring.'

'Reassuring?' she said bitterly.

'Of course. Think for a moment. If you were an agent trailing somebody, would you rush up to them in public and claim their acquaintance, thereby advertising the fact that you were there? Of course you wouldn't. You'd just keep discreetly out of sight, wouldn't you?'

She hesitated and then said reluctantly, 'I suppose so. But they're very cunning.'

'All right then. But if he was being cunning he'd hardly go and sit down at a chemmy table with his back to the exit, so that we could perfectly well have gone out without his seeing us. As it was, we had to go and stand slap in front of him for three banks before he even saw us. I give you my word—comrade Ferenic may or may not be a Communist agent, but at the moment he isn't interested in you. He's far more interested in winning a hell of a lot of money.'

Katherina said listlessly, 'You may be right. Anyhow, can we go now? I'm very tired.'

As we went out past the chemmy table, Ferenic was still playing. He had a big pile of very expensive looking plaques in front of him, and as we passed he was dealt cards, and with the invariable expression of wistful sadness showed an eight and an ace. He did not glance up at us, and as we made for the lifts I said to Katherina, 'That man doesn't need to be any sort of agent. All he has to do is to sit down at the big chemmy table and be dealt nine every time.'

There was the usual crowd of people waiting for the boat to take them back to Venice, but there were also a couple of taxi motor launches waiting for customers and I said, 'We'll take a taxi and damn the expense. And as you've won, you can pay for it.'

To my surprise she clutched the handbag that contained her winnings to her more closely and said, 'No—it is a waste of money.'

'Oh, come on—it'll only cost you three thousand lire and you've won about a hundred and twenty thousand this evening. With gambling, it ought to be easy come, easy go.'

'No,' she said doggedly. 'You gave me the money to play, and it is all yours if you want it. But you said it is mine, and if it is mine I shall not waste it.'

I said, 'And what are you going to do with it?' but remembered the night when Sarah had got five numbers running, and knew the answer in advance. I said, 'Don't bother to tell me—you're going to buy a handbag—or possibly three handbags.'

She looked at me sharply and said, 'Why do you say that?'

I said, 'When you get to my age, my dear, most of the things that are going to happen to you have happened before. There are about half a dozen good handbag shops in Venice, and to-morrow I will show them to you. In the meantime, we will take one of the taxi launches, and I will pay for it.'

As the launch dashed and bumped its way back across the lagoon to Venice Katherina suddenly said, 'Jim— I've got something that I must get clear with you.'

It always jarred when she called me Jim, just as it always jarred when I called her Sarah. Somehow the use of the Christian name brought home the falseness of the whole business. I said, 'Go right ahead, darling.'

She hesitated and then said, 'Well, so far, I've let you be in charge, and I've done what you've told me to do, even when I didn't agree with it. In fact I don't deny that it's been lovely to have somebody else in charge for once. But once we're in Yugoslavia, it will be different. You don't know the language or the country, or the people, and I do. You'll have to be prepared to take my word for things more than you've done so far, even if they're things that you don't understand.'

I had a vision of Popovic and his friends, sitting in Paris and being authorities on the country they hadn't visited for twenty years. I said, 'Of course there'll be things I don't understand, and then you'll be able to explain them to me, which will be fun for both of us.'

It was still only about eleven-thirty, but by unspoken consent we just went back to the hotel. I had thought that there might be awkward echoes of the previous night, but there were none. We went in turn to the bathroom, and undressed there with due propriety, and after that I sat and smoked whilst Katherina pottered about in her dressing-gown getting everything packed for our voyage on the following day. She took an uncommonly long time about it, and when she eventually went to her bed, it must have been about one o'clock.

I was deeply relieved that the previous night had been so quietly and tactfully forgotten, but nevertheless there was something missing, so I went over to her bed and kissed her on the cheek and said, 'Good night, darling,' and she said, 'Good night, Jim, and bless you.'

I was tired, and did not take long to go to sleep, but I remember hearing her tossing and turning restlessly, and I knew that she was thinking of Ferenic, and all the perils that lay before her.

9

THE trip from Venice across to Rijeka was an overnight affair, and we were not due to sail till eleven o'clock, though I had been warned to be there a couple of hours earlier, in order to see the car on board. This meant that we had the whole day to get through, and with Katherina obviously nervous and excited, the day seemed very long. I tried to get her to come for a walk, or to do some shopping with her gambling winnings, but it was obvious that she had had all she wanted of Venice for the moment, and in the end we spent most of the day sitting rather restlessly and silently in the Piazza San Marco, just waiting for it to be evening, when the real expedition could begin.

At one point when she had been silent for an unusually long time, Katherina suddenly said, 'About what I said on the boat last night, there are two or three things that I want to remind you about. And I want you to take them seriously, and not just laugh them off as you usually do.'

'Fire ahead.'

'Well, from now on we've got to be much more careful than we have been about how we talk to one another. Up till now we've acted as though I was your wife when we were in public, but not when we were by ourselves. From now on we've got to realize that we can never be sure that we *are* by ourselves.'

'There may always be a spy under the bed, eh?'

'There you are, you see. You think it's a joke, but it isn't. There probably won't be a spy under the bed, but there may perfectly well be a microphone. Popovic warned me that a lot of the rooms in the hotels which visitors are given are wired and have microphones in them. So never talk about anything that matters unless you're absolutely sure it's safe. Preferably outside, and when there's nobody anywhere near you. All the rest of the time, just act and talk as though we really were an English married couple on holiday. I know you hate calling me Sarah, but you must get used to it.'

'How do you know I hate it?'

'I just know.'

I said, 'If it comes to that, I hardly ever called Sarah Sarah, except when I was very angry with her. I usually called her "darling".'

'Well, that's all right. But anyhow, whatever you do, don't call me Katherina, even if you think we're quite alone.'

I said solemnly, 'Sarah darling, I can never remember having called you Katherina.'

'Then you said you had a friend at the British Embassy . . . ?'

'Yes. Willie Strang.'

'Will you want to go and see him?'

'It would be the normal thing to do.'

'How well does he know me?'

'Hardly at all. I think he's met you once for a few minutes several years ago. He certainly won't remember you, except vaguely.'

'Well, that's all right. But be very careful what you say to him. Embassy people talk a lot.'

'Willie Strang certainly talks a lot. He's one of those people who was inoculated with a gramophone needle.

To tell him anything would be the equivalent of putting it on the front page of the papers.'

Katherina stirred restlessly and stared at the pigeons for a long time and then said, 'And for the rest, you'll have to trust me. I may have to go and see people by myself . . . and things like that.'

'Why not? You're master-minding this whole operation. Once I've got you into the place, I hardly come into it until you want to get out again. After all, I'm hired to do as I'm told.'

That went right home. Her eyes suddenly filled with tears and she said rather chokily, 'Why do you have to spoil everything by saying beastly things like that?'

I said, 'That wasn't a beastly thing. I was only trying to say that from now on this is your show, and you must run it in your own way.'

I looked at the big, tear-filled grey eyes, and was reminded of the time in the hotel in Paris when I had told her to pull her frock down just when she had been at her most businesslike and dominant. There was the same sense that she was suddenly a very lonely and frightened girl, who was putting up a brave front but couldn't quite get away with it. I took her hand and said, 'Cheer up. Everything is going to be all right.'

She stared at me for a moment, and her lips opened as though she was going to say something. Then she bowed her head, and gripped my hand very tightly and muttered chokily, 'All right . . . ? You don't know. You don't know. . . .'

I said gently, 'I don't know what, darling?'

She gave a quick dab at her eyes and said, 'Oh, I don't know what I'm talking about, Jim. I hardly slept at all last night. and I'm just not making sense. Come on— let's go to Ciro and get you a drink. You must need it after all this nonsense.'

118

As far as one could judge from the quayside, everything about the ship looked smart and efficient. I believe she was sunk during the war and later re-floated, but one would never have guessed it to look at her, and they slung the little Alfa and lifted her on board quickly and skilfully. As we walked up the gangway I put my hand on Katherina's arm and found that it was trembling violently, and remembered that this was the first time for twenty years that she had stepped on to what was officially Yugoslav soil. Our tickets were examined by an officer who spoke Italian with a heavy Venetian accent. He also took our passports, and I saw the reluctance and fear in Katherina's face as she gave up that clumsy blue British passport of Sarah's, which meant so much more to her than it had ever done to its original owner. For here the whole world was requested and required in the name of Her Majesty to let her pass freely and without let or hindrance, and to afford her such assistance and protection as might be necessary; and to be allowed to pass freely and to be given the necessary assistance and protection was a thing that Miss Feldic had never known before. I think if she had had her way she would have slept with that passport strung around her neck.

We were shown down to a cabin which was neat and comfortable, but rather small. As soon as the door closed behind the man who had brought down our baggage, Katherina came close to me and said in a whisper, 'This is the sort of place where you must remember not to talk.'

Then she looked around and said aloud, 'Well, they don't give us much room, do they?'

I said, 'Oh, I don't know, darling—I think it's rather nice. And anyhow, it's only for one night.'

She said, 'Oh, yes—it doesn't matter, of course.' And

then looking around the cabin, and obviously addressing some invisible microphone, she said, 'It'll be funny to be in Yugoslavia again. Let's see, how long is it since we were there last?'

I said, 'Two years.'

'That's right,' she said brightly, still addressing her invisible microphone. 'So it is. Let's go up and watch the people coming on board.'

As we leant on the rail I said quietly, 'Look, darling— I fully understand about not saying anything in the cabin which isn't just small talk, but don't let's try to act it out too much, otherwise the dialogue gets bad and it all becomes a strain. Even if there is a microphone there, we don't have to perform to it all the time or we start sounding like a bad radio play.'

Katherina said nothing. She was staring intently at the passengers as they came aboard. I knew she was looking for Ferenic. I said, 'If you're looking for our friend, I'll bet he's sitting comfortably in the Casino making a lot of money at chemmy.'

The passengers were a mixed bag—half a dozen Americans, four middle-aged English women who looked as though they might be school teachers, a few Italians, and a surprising number of Germans or Austrians. Katherina insisted on going on watching until the gangway was pulled up, but there was no sign of Ferenic, and promptly at eleven o'clock we started down the lagoon, and left Venice behind us in all its glory in the bright moonlight. As we went below, the loud-speaker system was announcing in four different languages that the customs examination would take place at seven o'clock the following morning, and that we should parade, bringing with us any cameras, typewriters or binoculars.

There was a bar downstairs, and as we sat and drank

slivovitz I remarked that it seemed to be quite a civilized ship. Katherina at once said, 'Oh, this is just for the tourists to see, of course.'

She was rather silent and restless, and I guessed that she was thinking about the passport examination the following morning, so I said quietly, 'Now there's nothing whatever to worry about. We've got our passports and we've got our visas. We haven't even got any cameras, or typewriters or binoculars. There's no reason why they should be in the least interested in us, any more than they will be in the four school marms over there. The one thing to be careful about is not to understand if people talk to you in Serbo-Croat. That may be a bit tricky for you, but you did it very well with Ferenic. So cheer up and have another slivovitz.'

She nodded silently, and soon after said that she was tired, and we went down to the much suspected but probably quite innocent cabin, and went to bed in monosyllables.

§

The following morning we duly queued up for the customs and passport examination. There were two officials, both of whom spoke quite reasonable English. Like most minor officials of Communist countries, they were rather curt and off-hand in their dealing with the passengers, and the four English school mistresses, who each had a camera, were considerably flustered by having to write down lens and body numbers. But I could see that not a great deal of interest was taken in the actual passports, and I squeezed Katherina's arm reassuringly. She gave me a rather wan but gallant smile. Then it was our turn, and I laid my passport and Sarah's politely before the officer, who was a rather irritable man with a red face and bloodshot eyes. He took Sarah's passport and just for a moment he looked up at Katherina. But it was only for a moment, and then he thumbed through and found the visa, and then went through the same performance with my passport. He said curtly, 'Where are you going in Yugoslavia?'

I said, 'To Belgrade.'

'Why are you going there?'

'On holiday.'

'How long are you staying?'

'I'm not quite sure. Perhaps a week. Perhaps a little longer.'

'You have any Yugoslav money?'

'No. The only money I have is dollar travellers' cheques, and about ten thousand lire.'

'If you are British, why do you have dollar cheques?'

'Because we've just come from America.'

He stared at me for a moment with the bloodshot eyes as though he didn't believe me. Then he grunted and said, 'Any camera—typewriter—binoculars . . . ?'

'No.'

He stared at me again as though he didn't believe me and then, giving another grunt, stamped the two passports and shoved them abruptly back at me and waved us irritably out of the line. As we went out of the saloon I had my hand on Katherina's arm. I glanced at her and saw that she was very pale and that her eyes were closed.

I said, 'Well, that's that. He wasn't exactly the flower of courtesy, but still, it wasn't too bad.'

She opened her eyes and said contemptuously, 'He is a Croat peasant. They have no manners.' She suddenly slipped her hand into mine and squeezed it very hard and said in a low voice, 'Thank you, Jim.'

It was a beautiful morning with brilliant sunshine,

and the dark blue, clean clear waters of the Adriatic were flat calm. Opatija was in sight on our left, and beyond it, dead ahead, Rijeka. But it would be well over an hour before we docked, and we went and took deck-chairs up in the bows of the ship. Before we sat down, Katherina went and stared for a long time at the coast-line in silence, and I remembered that after all, this was her country, and she had not seen it since she was a child. When I remembered what I always felt on seeing Dover Castle again, after being out of England for only six months or so, I respected that silence.

As we settled into our deckchairs a couple of good-looking Yugoslav boys of about nineteen came by. They stared at Katherina with frank and obvious approval. One said something to the other in Serbo-Croat, and they both laughed, and the other replied, and they laughed again. Katherina gave a suppressed giggle, and I saw that she had gone slightly pink. I said, 'What was all that about?'

She hesitated for a moment and then said, 'Well, you see, they think I'm an English woman and don't understand Serbo-Croat, so they're talking—like boys of that age will.'

'What did they say?'

'Well . . . one said I had a nice figure—only that isn't exactly how he put it. And the other said he'd give a lot to be where this deck-chair is.' She added almost hurriedly, 'They don't mean any harm. They're only boys. But it's going to be a bit difficult this—hearing people speak a language that you know, and having to pretend that you don't understand. . . .' She was silent for a moment or two and then said almost to herself, 'Sarah Petersen . . . that's who I am. Sarah Petersen. An English tourist.'

There was a moment's silence while she gazed at the

coastline again and then I said, 'And what is it like to be Sarah Petersen? Because I've always wanted to know.'

She turned and stared at me for a long moment in silence. Then she gave a little shrug and said, 'It is like being a woman. Which is like not being a man. Which is a thing no man can understand.'

'Is it a happy feeling on the whole?'

'Oh, yes—very happy. Women are really very much alike. They always want the same things, and worry about the same things. If your Sarah were here, she would be feeling many of the things that I am feeling. She would be feeling, "I am not alone. I have with me a big handsome man, in all his power and glory. But I do not really understand him or know what he wants, and if I got it wrong he might go away. And then where should I be, with the whole man-made world against me?" '

I put out my hand and took hers and said gently, 'I give you my word that until this operation is over, I won't desert you. But why, oh why, Sarah, if you are a bit insecure, and are afraid that I might go away, do you constantly do things which might drive me away? Why did you come up to me at Barry's party, that last night in Hollywood, announcing that I was drunk when you know perfectly well that I wasn't, and spitting fire and brimstone because I was talking to Mary Gladstone?'

Katherina said, 'Mary Gladstone? She's the film-star with the forty-eight inch bust, isn't she?'

'Yes.'

'And horribly vulgar?'

'I suppose you could say that her films are vulgar. But she herself is quite a nice simple girl.'

'A nice simple girl with a forty-eight inch bust,' said Katherina thoughtfully. 'And I was angry, was I?'

'You were furious.'

'And very reasonably. Who wants her man to be talking to nice simple film-stars with forty-eight inch busts? You say that this was at a party?'

'Yes.'

'And had you talked to me at the party?'

'Yes—on and off. But you can't go to a party and just talk to your own wife. Anyhow, I made it up to you afterwards when we were driving home, by saying that you had been by far the most beautiful woman in the room, which was true.'

'Ah, yes—that would put it all right. . . . And then we made love, I expect?'

'Yes—we did.'

'Then what are you complaining about? I had only acted as any woman would.'

I said, 'All I'm complaining about is that the next day you were dead. That's all I ever have complained about. Dying like that is the only really unfair thing you've ever done to me. Opatija looks rather splendid from here. Do you know it? I thought it was a charming place.'

Katherina said, 'My father and mother used to go there.'

§

Opatija may be a charming place but there is nothing very much to be said for Rijeka, and we only stopped there long enough to get a cup of coffee and some money. Katherina said, 'Don't cash too much. I shall get you a much better rate on the black market when we get to Belgrade.'

There was a milling crowd in the bank, and we discovered that the previous morning, the dinar had been devalued, so that the rate for the dollar was now almost twice what I had expected. Katherina was cynically triumphant about this. She said, 'There you are, you see—that's the sort of thing the Communists are always doing. Quite suddenly everybody's money is only worth half what it was before.'

I said, 'It'll be very nice for us, because it doubles the value of our dollars.'

'It won't do you any good, you'll find. They'll just double the price of everything.'

§

From Rijeka to Belgrade is something like four hundred miles, but the little Alfa was splendidly lively, and we did the journey comfortably in two days. There was very little traffic, and the roads were much better than they had been when Sarah and I had last been in the country. I remarked on this to Katherina, and she said at once that the road to Belgrade had to be good because tourists would see it, but that in most other places the roads were shocking. Yet a little while later, when I remarked casually on the tumble-down condition of some of the peasant cottages, she immediately pounced on me and said that I didn't realize what Yugoslavia had gone through in the war.

I remember this as the pattern of the whole journey. Katherina was obviously torn between a tremendous pride in the country, its beauty and its traditions, and a dogged refusal to admit that anything could be right under a Communist government. If I admired, she brushed my admiration aside contemptuously. If I criticized, she immediately defended. The food, just as I had remembered it, was unpretentious but otherwise quite good. But when I said so, and added rather maliciously that I had not so far seen any of Popovic's little children dropping dead from starvation, she

126

became very angry, and informed me that I was just a tourist who didn't know what I was talking about.

On the second day we were lunching outside a little restaurant in a village or small town only about a hundred miles from Belgrade. The restaurant was on a corner, and a group of small children were playing just outside it. One of them dashed out into the road just as a car came round the corner rather fast. Katherina saw the danger and leapt to her feet and instinctively yelled a warning in Serbo-Croat. But she was too late. The car pulled up with screaming brakes and locked wheels, but not before the wing had caught the toddler and sent him head over heels into the gutter, where he lay spread-eagled, like a rag doll that somebody had thrown away. Then we were kneeling beside the child, who was unconscious, and I saw blood on the stone kerb, and blood streaming from a bad cut from his forehead, and realized that he had hit his head on the stone kerb in his fall. I thought for a moment that he was dead, but he was still breathing in quick gasps. I ran my hands over him, and couldn't find any obvious evidence of fractures. A small crowd had appeared from nowhere, and the driver of the car, a very fat man, was talking loudly and almost hysterically and gesturing, presumably explaining that it wasn't his fault. I said, 'I think it's mainly his head. Got anything we can use as a bandage?'

There was a fraction of a second's pause and then Katherina leapt to her feet and in what seemed a single movement, whipped up her skirt, tore a piece off her slip and started to fold it into a bandage. I shouted to the crowd at large, 'Get a doctor and an ambulance.' But all that happened was that the driver of the car continued to shout hysterically and a woman, who I think was the child's mother, rushed forward, wailing loudly as though to pick him up. I shouted urgently, 'No, don't move him,' and the woman hesitated for a second, understanding my gesture, if not my words. I said rapidly to Katherina, 'Tell them to get a doctor and an ambulance and not to move him until they come, in case he's damaged inside.'

She hesitated for a moment and then said in a quick low voice, 'But I mustn't speak Serbo-Croat here, otherwise they'll know. . . .'

I was furious and almost shouted, 'For God's sake—here's a kid who may be dying. Get on and tell them what to do. I can't, because they don't understand me.'

Once again for just a fraction of a second she hesitated, and then she took charge. She turned to the crowd and began to rattle out instructions in Serbo-Croat, in a curious dominant, almost contemptuous tone that a lady might use in talking to her servants.

The effect was magical. Here, clearly, was the voice of authority. All they had wanted was somebody to tell them what to do, and now somebody was telling them what to do in a language that they understood. Two men rushed off, one of them on a bicycle. The car driver ceased his hysterical shoutings, and the mother ceased her wailings and merely went on moaning. And meanwhile the little discarded rag doll lay there in the gutter with its blood seeping through what had been Katherina's slip.

Considering that we were in a village the doctor and the ambulance took very little time to arrive, and during that time Katherina remained, calmly and dominantly, in charge of the whole operation. But as they lifted the rag doll gently into the ambulance, she took my hand, pulled it urgently and said, 'Come on—we must get out of here.'

'Why?'

'Because the police will be here soon. I don't know

128

why they haven't been here already. And if they come and find me here, and hear that I speak Serbo-Croat, then they'll want to know why, and want to know a lot of other things too. And before we know where we are, they'll telephone Belgrade and . . . Come on, Jim. Come on! We've done all we can. Now let's get out quick.'

As the Alfa roared towards Belgrade I said, 'That was a very admirable performance.'

Katherina shrugged and said, 'What else could I do in the circumstances? But it's probably ruined me.'

'Why?'

'Well, you don't believe that there wasn't somebody amongst that crowd who'd take the number of the car, and report it to Belgrade? And say that the woman was obviously a Serb? There was an old man sitting there drinking beer at the restaurant. He kept looking at me in a curious way. I was just going to suggest that we should go when all this happened. Now, of course, he'll have seen the accident and seen everything that happened and heard me talking to them and he'll know that I'm not Sarah Petersen, and he'll telephone Belgrade and say so.'

'If we're talking about the same old boy—the one who was sitting at the corner drinking beer—he won't telephone anywhere. He doesn't realize the telephone's been invented yet. He must be at least ninety.'

Katherina sighed and said, 'Why do you do this? Do you think I don't know a police spy when I see one?'

I said, 'I'm sure you know a police spy when you see one. What worries me is that you see an awful lot of people who aren't police spies and think they are. Cheer up, darling. You did very well, and all you've lost is your slip.'

10

BELGRADE was very much as I remembered it—beautiful, but just a trifle drab and serious—the bread and butter of a city without the jam. My mind, for some reason, went back to Beverly Hills, where so much jam is crowded on to such a small piece of bread and butter. Katherina was very silent as we drove into the city, and I remembered that she was seeing it for the first time since she was a small child. She only spoke twice, at both times to point to a block of flats and say, 'That belonged to my grandfather.' Judging from the size of the blocks and their position, Katherina's grandfather must have been quite a property owner.

Our hotel was a rather splendid, nearly new building, obviously designed to attract Americans and other tourists—a sort of Belgrade-Hilton. As we stopped outside it Katherina said, 'Now remember—practically everybody in these hotels—receptionist and porters and people like that—are spies for the secret police.'

I said, 'I don't care if they're spies for the Conservative Party as long as they can find me a gents' lavatory, a whisky and soda, and cash me a travellers' cheque. They are my three essential needs for the moment.'

'All right. But don't cash any more cheques than you need for this evening. I can get you twice the official rate for dinars to-morrow.'

In the hotel, the first people we saw were two Americans who had been on the boat. They seemed to be having an argument with the cashier about the rate of exchange. Our bookings were in order, but there was a good deal of delay in finding anybody to take our luggage in, because the little hump-backed porter seemed to be carrying on a one-man strike against the management, and a loud row was going on. In the end he took our luggage, and more or less threw it into the lift, threw it out at the other end, threw it into our room and departed in a bad temper before I had time to tip him.

It was a large, quite pleasantly furnished room with a bathroom leading out of it. As soon as we were alone Katherina looked quickly around and put her finger to her lips in order to indicate the danger of hidden microphones. I had driven four hundred miles in two days and I was tired. I said, 'Yes, darling. I know,' and added as part of the script, 'Well, ha ha, here we are in Belgrade, eh? I'll be with you in a minute,' and shot into the bathroom.

About an hour later, when we had bathed and changed and generally felt a good deal fresher and better tempered, I said, 'And now what?'

Katherina came and sat close to me and said in the low voice that she used to defeat microphones, 'While you were bathing they sent a letter up for me. You see they've remembered to address it properly.' She handed me the envelope. It was addressed to 'Mr. and Mrs. J. Petersen.'

I said, 'Why Mr. and Mrs.?'

'It is usual to address letters to a married woman to both her husband and herself.'

'Anything important in it?'

'That I have to meet somebody as soon as I arrive. It is not far away, and I shan't be long.'

'You don't want me to come, or take you in the car?'

'No—I think it is better not.'

'Well, what I mainly want at the moment is a drink. As I remember it, there's a big place in this street called something Russian. What is it? The Moscow?'

'Yes. Moskva. It is very famous.'

'All right. Then I'll go there and have a drink, and you keep your date and then come and pick me up.'

'Very well. You said you wanted money changed. If you like to give me the cheques, I will change them now.'

'But can your friend change travellers' cheques?'

'He can change anything.'

All this was said in a sort of conspiratorial undertone. I gave her five hundred dollars in signed travellers' cheques, and she went and put the finishing touches to her face and went out saying, 'I will see you at the Moskva in about an hour.'

The Moskva was a big place, rather like a cross between an English pub and an old-fashioned French café. There was a good deal of red plush and gilt and mirrors, and all down one side of it were little wooden cubicles in which one could sit and drink in comparative privacy. They looked as though a good many assassinations and other Balkan political manœuvres had been hatched in them. I had forgotten about the cubicles, but now I saw them again I remembered sitting in one with Sarah and drinking beer and simultaneously the Serbo-Croat word for beer—*pivo*—came back to me. I bought myself a *pivo* and went to one of the cubicles from which one could see the door, and permitted myself the luxury of a few minutes' nostalgia about that last visit to Belgrade. It was fairly early and there were very few people in the place. I had nothing to do but wait for Katherina and think about the past. I could hear Sarah's voice saying, 'I *like* this country. It's a queer place, and rather grey and cold in the towns. But there's so much warmth out in the country, and anyhow, you feel that an awful lot has happened here.'

I must have been there nearly half an hour, in this fine mood of nostalgia, and I had finished my beer and gone to the counter for another when I saw Hardy. He was sitting at a table not far from the door, and he was exactly like one's recollection of Oliver Hardy of the Laurel and Hardy comedies—the same stout figure and slightly pouting face—even the same bowler hat. I think I noticed him because he wasn't *doing* anything. He wasn't smoking, nor drinking, nor reading a newspaper. He was just sitting there heavily, staring straight in front of him with an air which had something almost pathetically resigned about it—the sort of resignation that one has sometimes seen on the face of a bulldog, waiting for its master on a hot day. I reflected that Katherina would almost certainly say he was a member of the secret police, if only because of the bowler hat.

She was away about two hours, and then arrived looking very bright and animated. I held up a hand and she came over to the table and said, 'Hallo, Jim darling. Sorry I'm late,' in her best for-the-record voice and kissed me. As we sat down she passed me a big wad of notes under cover of the table and said quietly, 'Here's your money. I got four thousand three hundred to the dollar which is nearly twice the official rate.'

I slipped the awkward wad of notes into my jacket pocket and said, 'Well—how did it go?'

She looked so bright and cheerful that I expected her to say that everything had gone well, but instead she frowned and shook her head in a worried way and said, 'It's all rather difficult. My grandfather's been very ill again since they wrote to me.'

'Have you seen him?'

'Oh, no—he doesn't live in Belgrade any longer. He

133

lives in a village about ten miles outside. That's where we shall have to go when he's better.'

'Then who have you been seeing?'

She hesitated for a moment and then said, 'Vodanic. He's a heart specialist, and a very old friend of the family. He's the one who has sent me the letters. . . .'

At this moment the Oliver Hardy character in the bowler hat rose and made for the door with the air of a man who has finished some sort of rather boring stint. Katherina glanced round the room and said rather restlessly, 'I don't like this place. You can't talk here because you never know who is in the cubicle next door. Let's go somewhere else. Vodanic told me of a good restaurant, and you must be hungry.'

The restaurant was very small, but comfortable, with banquettes down its sides. We drank a slivovitz and then ordered some cevapcici—the little sausage things that one orders in tens, and of which I am particularly fond. I said, 'So what's the programme now?'

Katherina shrugged slightly and said, 'We shall have to wait a couple of days until my grandfather is better —that is, if he doesn't die, which he perfectly well might. Then we shall have to go out to the village to see them.'

'And collect the stuff?'

'No. We only do that just before we leave, and we must stay at least a week, otherwise it won't look as though we've come on holiday.'

The cevapcici were delicious, and I was just turning to Katherina to remark on it, so that I was looking full at her, when suddenly I could have sworn that her face lit up and her lips parted slightly as she gazed towards the door. I followed her glance and saw that a man had just entered. He was about my own height, which is exactly six feet, and very handsome, with the high cheek bones and the well-cut nose of a typical Serb. His eyes were striking—large and an almost enamel blue, like a Siamese cat's. I judged him to be in the late thirties. I looked again at Katherina but her eyes were on her food and she said casually, 'These are good, aren't they?'

The Serb conferred briefly with the waiter and was then brought over to sit on the banquette on our right, so that he was only a few feet away from us. As he was shown to his place Katherina muttered under her breath, 'Damn! Now we can't talk any more.'

I said in my public voice, 'Well, what would you like to do to-morrow, darling?'

And Katherina said, 'I thought we might go up to that place by the Danube—you know, the Park with the Fortress. What's it called . . . ?'

I said, 'That's fine with me. How about some more cevapcici? Can you do another ten?'

We had finished the meal and were waiting for our coffee when I lit a cigarette. The big Serb on my right leaned over and said politely, 'Excuse me—can you oblige me with a light?'

His English was excellent, but with just a trace of an American accent. I lit his cigarette for him and he thanked me and added with a smile, 'It is a great pleasure to hear English spoken again.'

I said, 'Have you been in England?'

'In England—no, except to pass through. But I was in America for several years. My name is Petrov. Jovan Petrov.'

I said, 'James Petersen. And this is my wife Sarah.'

They nodded to one another briefly and Petrov said, 'Will you join me in a slivovitz?'

'That's very kind of you. What were you doing in America?'

'I was lecturing at a university,' Petrov said rather vaguely.

'You are a Yugoslav?'

He smiled and said, 'I am a Serb.'

Katherina said, 'Did you like America?'

He stared at her for a moment with the enamel-blue eyes and said, 'In some ways very much. In others no. It is strange to find a country so advanced technically and so politically immature.' He gave a slight shrug and then added, 'But then—all countries are politically immature.'

I said, 'Including Yugoslavia?' I felt Katherina's knee pressing hard against mine, and knew that I was being warned not to get into a political discussion. Petrov shrugged again and said, 'Yugoslavia is a special case, with special problems of her own. But at least here we realize that politics are important, and a thing to be thought about, and not to be settled by merely emotional decisions, full of brass bands and drum majorettes. I would not claim that the Slav is politically mature, but at least he is politically conscious. You are here on holiday, Mr. Petersen?'

'Yes.'

'Do you or your wife speak Serbo-Croat?'

'I'm afraid not.'

'Nor understand it?'

'No. Except for a word here or there.'

'That's a pity. It is difficult to understand Yugoslavia unless you speak the language. It is not really a beautiful language. Not as beautiful, for example, as Russian. But it has some things to recommend it.' He smiled and spoke for a few seconds in voluble Serbo-Croat, and I noticed while he did so the enamel-blue eyes were on Katherina, and not on me. Katherina listened with the same polite lack of comprehension that she had used when Ferenic had talked to her in Serbo-Croat in the Casino in Venice. She really did this very well. Petrov said, 'You see, it is

rather a harsh language, not a soft one like Russian or
Italian.' He drained his slivovitz, signalled for his bill
and said, 'Well—I must go. It has been delightful to
meet you, Mr. and Mrs. Petersen. I hope we shall meet
again sometime.'

When he had gone I said to Katherina. 'That was a
nice young man—and a good-looking one too. What was
it he said in Serbo-Croat?'

She said, 'Oh, just something about hearing us say
that we were going to the park to-morrow and that he
hoped we should look at the Danube and be very happy.'

THE next couple of days should have been pleasant
enough, since we had nothing to do but potter about in
and around Belgrade and the weather was very beautiful. We went to the Kalimegdan gardens and to Avala,
and one night we went up to the golf club and dined on
the terrace with fireflies shimmering in the darkness
beyond us, just as Sarah and I had done. Yet a vast black
depression had descended on me, and try as I might, I
could not shake it off. It was partly due to Katherina.
Every evening she went off for a couple of hours about
her own mysterious affairs and came back seemingly
refreshed and in high spirits. But for the rest of the time
she was tense, strained, and usually in a bad temper.
Somehow her conviction that our bedroom was not a
safe place to talk in made everything very cold and
distant, and though I had no particular desire to be so
very close to her, I found occupying a bedroom with a
young woman with whom you can exchange nothing
but small talk an increasing strain and increasingly
unpleasant. I seemed much further from her than I had
in Venice, or even in the Hotel St. Jacques in Paris.
When she went off on her own, I resented it and was
bored sitting drinking beer in a Yugoslav café, and
when she came back obviously revived by what she had
been doing, I resented that too. Somehow I seemed to
have no function in the whole matter, and with that
feeling there came back the black hell of loneliness and

futility and dread of the future. I used to wake up at exactly three o'clock each morning, and lie awake for a couple of hours wishing to be dead, and seeing the wing dip and that fiery cart-wheel on the runway at Los Angeles, and going through all that has happened afterwards, with its atmosphere of cold despair. As in Venice, when this happened, I had to sit up in bed and switch the light on to get rid of the terrors of the darkness, and there she would be—Katherina sleeping peacefully, as Sarah might have slept, but dreaming her queer little Serbian dreams of riches, and a real passport of one's own, and never having to type any more—never, never. But though the sight of her there would reassure me somewhat—enough to enable me to put out the light and perhaps to go to sleep—I desperately wanted more. It was not only that I wanted to make love to her, though God knows I sometimes wanted that too. It was that I wanted to be a part of some relationship, rounded, complete, and taking everyday existence for granted, without eternally questioning the point of it. And this, during those few days in Belgrade, was what she never gave me. The moods were still there—the sulks, the periods of extreme cheerfulness, the suspicions, and so on. But they were all to do with her own strange private affairs, and nothing to do with me. I was a stranger in a strange land, with nothing to mitigate the cold sense of emptiness.

It was therefore a great relief to me when on the evening of the third day after we reached Belgrade she came back in high spirits and said that her grandfather was much better, and that we could go and see her grandparents the following evening. The village was called Malo Selo, and it was about ten miles out of Belgrade. As we drove out, Katherina said, 'I haven't prepared you for this, and I'm not really very prepared for it myself. Their house was the biggest one in the village, and I used to stay there when I was a small child. It was the one that had the vineyard, but now they're only allowed two rooms, because there are three other families in the house. So I expect it'll all be rather odd.' She sighed and said, 'My poor darling little grandmother. She's only about five feet high, but for the last twenty-five years she must have been going through hell. The village is on the main road to the east, and on the main railway line. It was quite a big station, and that's where the Simplon makes its last stop before it gets to Belgrade. During the war years my grandmother had soldiers billeted in her house six times—the Germans coming and the Germans going, and then both lots of partisans, and then the Russians coming and the Russians going. And now, after all that, when she's seventy-five, they only let her have two rooms, and she has to nurse my grandfather who is nearly ninety and practically helpless. Not that he had an easy war either. It wasn't far from here that my father died. He was fighting with the Mihailovic partisans and the Communists took him prisoner and shot him out of hand. Then they made my grandfather come and identify the body. My father was his only son.' She said it dully and without visible emotion.

I said gently, 'And your mother . . . ?'

'Oh, she was killed by the Germans earlier on,' said Katherina in the same dull, matter of fact way. 'I don't know any of the details of that. Perhaps it's just as well. You see, there were so many different lots of people that you could get yourself killed by in Yugoslavia during the war.'

We were coming into the village now—or perhaps one should call it a small town. Most of it had been knocked down during the fighting, and had been replaced by new buildings, which were in that curious style, at once modern and rather dull, that I had seen in places in Belgrade. I noticed in particular a sort of large café-cum-restaurant which had a big neon sign over it which spelt out the word 'Nylon'. Loud canned music was coming from it. On the opposite side of the road was a sort of public garden—quite pretty, with a lot of rose trees in it. Katherina said, 'The station is down there, and where that garden is used to be the road to it. But when the Communists took over, they decided to show everybody how clever they were and how they were going to brighten the place up. So they took the station road and turned it into a garden, which means that you can't get to the station any longer except on foot. My grandmother wrote to me and told me about it.' She added with bitter contempt, 'The fools! The house is down here on the left—at least that's how I remember it.'

The house was in a prominent position in the middle of the main street. It was a sizeable place of Victorian design painted white, but not as big as I had expected from what Katherina had said. The same thought occurred to her, because as we stopped the car and got out she said, 'Odd how one remembers places as being much bigger than they really were. I remember this place as being huge, and having a garden the size of a public park. But then I haven't seen any of it since I was seven. Now let's see—I think we go in the gate here and round to the back and then up some steps. . . . The old people are on the first floor now.'

We went through a side gate and into the garden. It was about thirty yards square, very pleasant and surprisingly well kept. A rather rickety set of wooden stairs led up to the first floor, and Katherina's grandmother was standing at the top of them to greet us. When Katherina saw her she gave a sort of little groan and said, 'Oh, darling . . .' and ran up the steps and clutched the little figure at the top of them.

My first reaction to Katherina's grandmother was that she really was remarkably small. Not only was she about five feet high, but she was so thin and frail that one felt that if one were to touch her slightly roughly, she would simply dissolve into dust like a mummy. I had been told that she was seventy-five, but I judged that she was older than that. There was not an atom of flesh on her anywhere, and her face was simply swarthy brown skin drawn tight over some splendid bones, and her hand was a skeleton's hand. All that was left of her which was not a skeleton was a pair of very fine dark, slightly hooded eyes. Yet there was something magnificently dignified about her, and as Katherina introduced us and she offered me gracefully her claw-like hand, I saw the courage and pride in the tilt of her head and realized where Miss Katherina Feldic had got at least some of her characteristics. Katherina said, 'This is going to be a bit difficult for you. My grandmother only speaks Serbo-Croat.'

I said, 'Then tell her that we shall just have to make love with our eyes.'

Katherina translated and this went down very well. The old lady positively bridled with pleasure and immediately addressed me volubly in Serbo-Croat. The big dark hooded eyes occasionally went to Katherina, and at a long guess I decided that I was being told that the old lady had not seen her for many years, and what a beautiful woman she had become.

I said, 'Yes,' at a venture and then when the old lady shook her head bravely and sadly, I too shook my head and said, 'No.' Throughout our visit she sometimes turned and talked to me in this way, completely ignoring the fact that I could not understand a word of what she was saying. But she had a most expressive face, and at least I could usually guess whether something had made

142

her glad or sad and answer 'Yes' with a bright smile or 'No' with a solemn shake of the head. When she paused I said to Katherina, 'Does your grandmother know about us? I mean . . . ?'

'Oh, yes. She knows all about it. That's what she's just been saying—how grateful she is to you.'

We went inside. There was a sort of little entrance hall with a stove in it and two or three chairs. It must have been about nine feet square. Katherina said, 'This is one of the rooms they have. The other is the bedroom. My grandfather is asleep at the moment, but he will wake up soon.'

The old lady turned to me and asked me what was obviously a question. I caught the one word 'slivovitz' and drawing a bow at a venture nodded and said, 'That would be very kind of you.' She seemed pleased and nodded and went away.

Katherina said, 'I'm sorry—this is going to be horribly boring for you. There isn't much I can do about it. I gather that my grandfather speaks a very little English. He taught himself by reading an English dictionary. But as he started when he was about seventy, I doubt whether he's very good.'

I said, 'Don't worry. This is what I came here for. Your grandmother's magnificent.'

Katherina was pleased and said, 'She is rather splendid, isn't she? She likes you. She says she always did like big, handsome men.'

Grandmother came back with a tray on which there were a bottle with no label, three glasses and a plate with some spring onions and salami. She put it down on the table, muttering something to Katherina, who said, 'My grandmother wants you to consider yourself one of the family and to help yourself.'

I poured out a glass of slivovitz for each of them, and

143

was just pouring one for myself when the old lady started to fumble in the front of her dress and produced a rather battered packet of Serbian cigarettes. I took one for courtesy's sake, and was surprised to see her produce a modern ejector holder, fit a cigarette into it and light it with every appearance of satisfaction. Katherina said, 'She smokes all the time. She oughtn't to, because of her heart. But there it is.'

I placed a chair for the old lady, and she thanked me with a flash of the hooded eyes and sank down into it and sat there, smoking her cigarette and sipping her slivovitz and talking to Katherina in her rather deep slow voice, as complete an example of a well-bred lady doing a little casual entertaining as I have ever seen. For my part, I tried the slivovitz and the salami and found them delicious. They were apparently both local products.

I don't know how long they talked. Perhaps for about an hour. During that time the room gradually became darker, but nobody suggested switching on a light. I only remember that during that gathering dusk, sitting and eating salami and onions and drinking slivovitz, and listening to a conversation which I could not understand, I was for a short time supremely happy. I could even think, quite calmly and objectively, that I wished Sarah had been there. It was the sort of moment that she understood and would have appreciated. But magical moments never last long enough, and all too soon the old lady, who had been sitting absolutely still in her chair, shifted a little, put out her cigarette and said something to Katherina, and Katherina turned to me and said, 'She thinks that my grandfather will be awake now, and that we should go and see him.'

We went into the inner room. It was quite a large room, and it would have looked a good deal larger if it had not contained a full-sized grand piano, placed with its key-board jammed up against the wall, so that there could be no question of anybody playing it. Apart from the grand piano there were two or three pieces of French style furniture, gilded and upholstered in light-blue velvet, three kitchen chairs and a night stool. These all stood on a splendid big Keshan carpet. Katherina's grandfather was lying propped up in a big double bed. He was a huge, very heavy old man, and the bulge of his belly was visible even through the bedclothes. It was a warm evening, but all the windows were closed, and though the room was scrupulously clean, it smelt of a queer mixture of things, of which perhaps the prevailing one was the strange sickly-sweet smell of old people.

I think old Mr. Feldic had only just awoken, because he blinked at us uncomprehendingly, and then, taking no notice of Katherina and myself, spoke angrily and complainingly to his wife. The old lady went over and patted his hand and smoothed down his pillows. Then she said something to him and indicated Katherina. For a moment he went on blinking at us vaguely, and then his whole puffy old face with its small rather pig-like eyes lit up, and he held out both arms to her and hugged her to him, and slobbered vaguely at her cheeks. This took a long time. Then Katherina presented me and he held out his hand and said very formally, 'How do you do?'

We shook hands and I said, 'You speak English, sir?'

The old man shook his big head and said, 'No. No speak. I have book and I read. Very good English book.'

Katherina said quietly, 'He only started to teach himself when he was over seventy.' She spoke to him gently in Serbo-Croat, stroking his hand. He answered her for a moment or two, and then his voice broke and he began to cry. The tears poured down his cheeks as he went on speaking in a hoarse broken voice, and he clung to Katherina's hand desperately. The old lady and I just stood there, and she caught my eye, and gave a little shrug, and said something to me in a low voice in Serbo-Croat. Old Mr. Feldic was clinging to Katherina's hand, and he pulled her head down to his mouth and whispered in her ear urgently. As he did so, his spittle was going all over her face. She nodded and spoke to him gently and reassuringly and nodded towards me. The whole of the big pig-eyed face suffused with joy, and he held her to him and slobbered more kisses over her face. When he released her, Katherina turned to me and said, 'He wants me to tell you how grateful he is to you for helping me. He's very anxious for me to have the things that he's kept for me.'

The old man gestured towards me and said, 'Good. Very good. I have. I give. Katherina takes. Good.'

In English, verbs seemed to be his strong suit.

They went on talking for some time—the huge bulky old man eagerly, and Katherina soothingly and gently. Old Mrs. Feldic sat down firmly in one of the blue velvet upholstered chairs, took a cigarette out of her bosom and put it in the holder and lit it. There was nothing that I could do, so I went and sat beside her, and she put out a curious brown claw of a hand and took mine, and looked at me with those very big dark eyes and gave me a reassuring nod. After she had been kissed some more, Katherina turned to me and said, 'Look—this must be all very boring for you. Why don't you go into the other room and have another slivovitz, and leave me to cope?' She turned and spoke to the old man and he immediately said, 'Good day. Yes. Thank you. Good day,' and held out a trembling hand to me which I shook.

I went out into the other room and poured myself another slivovitz, and looked at the fireflies in the garden and reflected, with fine originality, what a stange thing love is, and how many different forms it takes. I must have sat there for about half an hour. Then Katherina came out of the inner room and said, 'The old boy's just relieving himself. Luckily he remembered to ask this time. Usually nowadays he just wets the bed. When he's finished my grandmother's going to show us the stuff.' She sighed and said, 'It's an awful thing to be as old as that. He used to be a very able man.'

I said, 'He's obviously very fond of you.'

'Oh, yes. But he's completely gaga now. He keeps talking about the vineyard. You know I told you that he exchanged it for a diamond. Well, sometimes he remembers that he hasn't got it any longer and sometimes he doesn't. He keeps saying I must have the diamond and that he got it for me, and then he goes back and says it will be nice for me to have the vineyard, because then I shall have plenty of apricots. You see he remembers that I was fond of apricots.' Her voice broke slightly and she blinked hard and said, 'Give me a slivovitz, for God's sake.'

I gave her a glass of the local slivovitz, with its strange taste of boot polish, and she drank it at a gulp.

A few minutes later the old lady opened the door and beckoned to us silently. We went into the inner room. As soon as the old man saw me he said, 'Good day. Yes. Good day,' and held out his hand. As I shook it he turned to his wife and was obviously asking who I was. Katherina spoke to him rather sharply and irritably, and he immediately nodded the big head with its puffy face and small eyes.

The old woman muttered something to Katherina, and going across to the grand piano, lifted its lid with something of an effort and took out of its interior a canvas bag. She brought it across to the bed, fumbled with its strings for a moment and then poured out on to the bed a tinkling shower of gold pieces. She looked from Katherina to me and held out her brown claw of a hand towards the gold in silence. It was quite a big bag and at a guess I should say there may have been five hundred pieces there. They were mainly English sovereigns and half sovereigns, though some had that slightly greenish tint which suggested that they might have been Australian. The rest were mainly gold Napoleons, some of them apparently from Austria. I am not up to date with gold prices, but at a rough guess I should have said that what was on the bed was worth somewhere between two and three thousand pounds. Katherina said to me, 'Of course, it's quite illegal for them to have it, and if it were ever found they would certainly go to prison, and quite probably be shot. They've got nowhere to keep it here, and they're terrified of burglars. That's one of the reasons why they want me to have it.

I said, 'And very nice too. The question is how do we get it out?' I glanced at the old man and saw that he was gazing at the gold coins with something like ecstasy. He was dribbling slightly, and I was reminded vividly of a large dog drooling over a plate of meat that he can see but has been forbidden to touch.

The old lady scooped up the gold coins in a matter of fact way and poured them back into the bag. She lifted the lid of the piano again and replaced the bag, and then brought out what looked like three one pound cocoa tins, and said something to Katherina. Katherina said, 'This is her jewellery.'

The old lady took the lids off the cocoa tins and poured the contents willy-nilly on to the bed. As I looked at it, my heart sank. Jumbled together like that, it naturally did not look its best. But one did not need to be an expert to see that most of the stuff was old-fashioned, and not of very high quality. The main item, clearly, was a big solitaire diamond ring—presumably the one for which the old man traded the vineyard. I was just putting out my hand to pick it up and examine it when he suddenly made a grab for it and held it to his chest protectively. Katherina spoke to him in the sharp, irritable way that she had done before, and he slowly gave it up, reluctantly and guiltily, like a child who is giving up a sweet that it has stolen. Katherina almost snatched it away from him and handed it to me. It was a big stone of some seven or eight carats, and if it had been better cut and of a better colour it might have been worth a lot of money. But as it was, it was lifeless and glassy. I remembered a shop just off the Charing Cross Road in London which specializes in big cheap diamonds. They might give you a thousand pounds for it, but not more. And thereafter it would remain in their window for years at a price of fifteen hundred pounds. I put it down and said, 'Very beautiful.'

Apart from that there was a big emerald, badly flawed and not of a good colour, a pleasant enough sapphire bracelet, and a diamond necklace of rose diamonds. The rest consisted of the sort of things that a woman may accumulate during a long lifetime—charm bracelets, and necklaces of semi-precious stones, and pairs of small diamond ear-rings, and a lot of rings which were charming enough, and probably worth about fifty pounds each. I did a rough calculation as I looked through the items, and decided that had I been a London dealer I might have given Mrs. Feldic five thousand pounds for the lot. But certainly not a penny more.

They were all three watching me closely as I examined the jewellery items, so I turned to Katherina and said, 'Your grandmother has some very pretty things here.'

It seemed inadequate, but I did not know what else to say. The old lady said something to Katherina and went to the door. Katherina said, 'She has something else she wants to show you.'

The old woman came back carrying a big heavy box of wood and threw it open to display a vast dinner service in continental silver—one of those old-time dinner services for twenty-four people. She spoke rapidly to Katherina. Katherina said, 'She wants you to have that, because you are being so kind.'

I had a vision of myself trying to smuggle half a hundredweight of bad continental silver out of the country, and I turned and took the curious brown claw, squeezed it hard and looked into those magnificent dark eyes, and kissed the curious leather cheek, and knew as I did so that I had done the right thing. The old man laughed and said, 'Yes. Good. I have. She have.' He pointed to Katherina and started to cry again. He cried in great gasps, with the tears pouring down from the little pig-like eyes to the fat puffy cheeks. The old lady scooped up the jewellery and put it back in the cocoa tins and put them back in the piano. Katherina said, 'Well, I should think you've had quite enough of this. Go back to your slivovitz, and I'll be with you in a few moments.' As I got up the old man stopped his vast sobs and said, 'Good day. Good day,' and held out the tremulant hand. I shook it and said:

'Good day, sir,' and went out.

§

When we left we drove for some while in silence. Then Katherina said, 'I am very grateful to you for that.'

I said, 'What for? I didn't do anything.'

'Perhaps not. But you were nice to them. Apart from

that there wasn't anything you *could* do. Nor that I can, for that matter. . . .'

She gave a little shudder and said, 'You can't think how horrible it is to see them like that, when I remember . . . what things used to be like for them. It seems awful to take anything away from them when they're already in that state. Yet they both keep insisting that I should have it and that they'd be very much happier if I did.'

'I think one can understand that, perhaps,' I hesitated and then said, 'My dear—there's a thing I've got to say to you. I hate to do it, but I must. . . . How much do you think that stuff is worth?'

'I don't know. I'm no good at that sort of thing. But it must be a lot, with the gold and all the diamonds and so on. How much do *you* think?'

I said, 'I'm no expert. Of course the gold's all right, if we can think of a way of getting it out. But the jewellery . . . well, it's worth quite a bit of course, but it isn't exactly a fortune you know.'

There was a moment's silence and then she said quietly, 'How much?'

'Well, as a pure guess—probably about five thousand pounds.'

'But how about that big diamond? He sold the vineyard for that alone.'

'I don't know what the vineyard was worth, and certainly if a diamond of that size was a good stone it would be worth a lot of money. But that *isn't* a very good stone, and selling things like that is always tricky.'

There was a long pause. Then she said, 'How much is five thousand pounds in francs?'

'About sixty-five thousand. Then there's the gold, which is probably worth another thirty or forty thousand, so that at a rough guess the whole lot is worth something round seven or eight thousand pounds, or about a hundred thousand francs.'

She said nothing, so I added, 'I'm only telling you this because I don't want you to be disappointed later. A hundred thousand francs is quite a lot, of course, but I thought you might be expecting a lot more, from the way you talked about it in Paris.'

'Of course I was expecting more,' she said with a sudden spurt of irritation. 'But what's that got to do with it? They're very old, and they can't be expected to know. This is all they've got, and it looks a lot to them. How much do I owe you?'

'That depends how we reckon it.'

'No, it doesn't. You said three thousand dollars a week, and then there's all the money you've spent and given me and buying this car and so on. . . . When I've paid all that back, will there be anything left?'

'Oh, yes—of course. But . . .'

'Then that's all right,' she said calmly, 'As long as there's enough to pay you back and get me back to Paris, nothing else really matters.'

The tranquillity with which she said it left me rather puzzled. I had expected loud protests, and even tears. I said, 'That's all very well, darling, but it isn't what you were hoping for when you came here, is it? You were talking about . . .'

'Never mind what I was talking about or hoping for,' she said curtly. 'There's never any harm in hoping for things, is there?'

I could not help admiring the calmness and courage with which she was facing a bitter disappointment. But looking back now, I can see that the whole tone of this conversation made me slightly uneasy. Somehow it was all slightly too good to be true. After all, the whole object of the expedition had been to collect this money and jewellery, and she had talked expansively about there being, 'plenty for everybody,' and how she would live on it in comfort for the rest of her life. This might just be characteristic Slav exaggeration. But from what I had seen of her, Miss Katherina Feldic was certainly a person who desperately wanted the things that money could buy her, and I was puzzled by this new attitude which was not only brave but almost nonchalant. Knowing how secretive and suspicious she was, I could not help wondering whether there was something here that was being kept from me. The only thing I could think of was that perhaps the old people had far more resources than had been shown to me, and that the idea was to avoid paying me a share in a much larger sum. But here again, this seemed unlikely from what I had seen of her, since she had always been most careful to keep a note of every dollar she had had from me. In short, I felt vaguely that there was something wrong somewhere, but could not for the life of me think what it could be. I felt, as I had felt ever since we came to Yugoslavia, that we were a very long way apart, and cursed my lack of knowledge of Serbo-Croat that reduced me to a dummy, sent into the next room to drink slivovitz whilst the vital conversations were going on.

It was only about nine o'clock when we reached Belgrade, and Katherina at once said that she didn't want any dinner, and had some people to see. She suggested that I should have dinner and meet her later at the Moskva. I dined alone, briefly and rather unhappily and went to the Moskva to wait for her. The place was full and I noticed that the Oliver Hardy character in the bowler hat was present. As before, he neither drank nor smoked nor read. He just sat alone, staring into vacancy. At about ten-thirty Katherina arrived, and I knew as she walked across to my table with the nervous swagger which always reminded me so vividly of Sarah that something had happened. She greeted me with the usual loud, 'Hallo, Jim darling,' and the usual kiss for public purposes, and then as we sat down she said in a low voice, 'Be careful what you say. There's a man over there who is a police agent.'

I said, 'You don't by any chance mean the fat man in a bowler hat?'

'Yes. How do you know?'

'I've seen him here before. A man who looks like that and wears that hat *has* to be a police agent—in a slapstick comedy. In real life he's probably a fishmonger.'

'When I left the hotel this evening, he was in the hall, talking to the manager. He followed me.'

'What did you do?'

'I . . . I shook him off. It was quite easy. But now here he is again. There you are, you see—he's going now.'

The Oliver Hardy character was making for the door. I said, 'What makes you think he's a police agent? No sane police force would employ a man like that, whom anybody would recognize.'

'He was in the hotel. And then he followed me. And then here he is again.'

'But I tell you—he often comes here. He was here for half an hour before you came, and now you've come, he's gone. As for having been in the hotel—why shouldn't he be? It seems to me that he might just as well feel that you're a police agent and following him.'

She sighed and said with infinite weariness, 'Oh, God, I wish you wouldn't do this flippant stuff about serious things.'

I said, 'I absolutely refuse to take Oliver Hardy seriously. That man couldn't trail a blind rhinoceros without being spotted. Forget him. He's just an ordinary

154

citizen who's now gone home to his wife and children. How did you get on with your friends?'

'Quite well. They think we should give it another two or three days and then go.'

'Go how? By train, or boat, or car, or what?'

She shrugged and said, 'They do not know. They're all dangerous. But since we have the car, probably by car.'

I said, 'How wrong can you be? If there is one way of making sure that you're searched from head to toe it's to take a car across a border.'

'Of course you know better.'

'I think I probably *do* know more about passing borders than most of your friends. The trouble is that damned gold. It's heavy, awkward stuff. The jewellery is easy enough if we use our brains.'

She said sarcastically, 'I don't doubt that the great brain will find a way of dealing with the situation.'

This was a mistake, because it got under my skin. I said, 'Listen, young woman. Just one more sneer out of you and I walk out on this whole thing and leave you flat and you and your precious friends can sort it out. For some curious reason—presumably because you look like my wife—I wanted to help you when we were in Paris and in Venice. But since we've been here it's been nothing but this exaggerated cloak and dagger nonsense and I'm tired of it. You're still reminding me of my wife —in her very worst phases, when nobody could do anything right for her, and there was nothing to be got out of it except a kick in the teeth. Now either snap out of it and let me help you, or to-morrow I just walk out of here and go back to Paris and leave you to go it alone.'

I knew there were only two possibilities—that she would reply defiantly and angrily or that she would cry.

155

I was looking at her closely and my heart sank as I realized that she knew this too and was deciding which to do. She took too long about it, and when she decided to cry, I knew finally and conclusively that Miss Katherina Feldic was not playing straight with me. Those beautiful big grey eyes filled with tears and she said in a broken voice, 'Jim—I'm sorry. It's been a rather upsetting day. But don't leave me now. I need your help. I'm sorry if I've been bitchy but . . .'

I took her hand and said dully, 'That's all right. We all need one another's help. But we're partners, aren't we?'

She said, 'Yes,' in a low voice and squeezed my hand, but I knew that we weren't really partners, and I didn't see why.

That night, after we had gone to bed and put the lights out, I was nearly asleep when I heard the rustle of her getting out of bed, and realized that she was standing beside mine. I said, 'What is it, darling?'

She said in a low voice, 'Jim—I'm lonely. Can I come to bed with you?'

I suddenly remembered that I had heard that line before somewhere. It was when Sarah had been having an affair with Matthew Gilder and had got a bit frightened about it. I said, 'Wait a minute . . . Let's put on the lights and have a look at you.'

I switched the lights on and there she stood in the nightdress I had told her to buy in Paris, just exactly as Sarah had looked in the hotel in New York. Infinitely seductive, infinitely ready to make a bargain, infinitely guilty. I put out an arm and pulled her down into the bed with me and switched the light off and said, 'You little cheater, Sarah. That's what you are. You're a little cheater. If I have any more of it I'll beat you till you can't sit down.'

She said, 'Why do you call me a cheater? How am I cheating?'

'That's what I don't know. But I've had enough experience of the likes of you to know when you're up to something.'

She said nothing but merely clung to me. I said, 'Would you like to tell me about it?'

There was a pause and then she said in a flat voice, 'There's nothing to tell.'

'So this is just a burst of spontaneous affection, is it?'

'Affection and . . . gratitude. You were sweet with my grandparents and I'm grateful. That's all. You don't have to do anything about it if you'll hate it to-morrow morning.'

I whispered, 'Be quiet, darling. You're forgetting that microphone.'

I made love to her. It was a queer, rather unsatisfactory business, not at all as it had been in Venice. Half of me wanted her desperately, but the other half had its reservations now. That half was puzzled and slightly wary. I think she sensed this because later, when I was lying physically satisfied and rather sleepy, she gave me a last gentle kiss and then slipped out of the bed and went back to her own.

12

THERE was no shyness or sense of guilt the following morning, as there had been in Venice. Then, what I had done had half seemed a betrayal of something precious. Now all that had happened was that I had been given the chance to go to bed with a beautiful young woman, and had done so. There was no confusion this time with anything I had ever felt about Sarah, or any feeling that she was at all concerned in the matter. Somehow Miss Katherina Feldic was now a person in her own right, not merely a part of an optical illusion, and the realization of this came as a tremendous relief to me. I could now be Katherina's lover if I wanted to without all the undertones which had previously made everything complicated. We went up to Avala again and giggled happily over the menu, which offered us, amongst other things, 'Hamm and egs'.

Whilst we were lunching I said, 'Look, we've got to have some sort of a plan about how we're going to get that stuff out of the country. Remember that for this purpose we're just British tourists, and I doubt they'll be very interested in us, any more than they were when we came in. As far as the jewellery goes, you can just wear some of it, stick the rest in a jewel case, and who's to know it isn't your own? But the gold is a bit difficult, mainly because it's so heavy. I think everything depends on how we're going back. The way we came? or take the car and drive all the way? or abandon the car and go by train? or even fly?'

She said nothing, and I glanced at her and saw that

her eyes were looking away across the room, and realized that she wasn't really listening to anything that I was saying. I said, 'What do you think?'

Katherina said rather vaguely, 'I don't really know. I'd rather leave it to you.'

Once again I was surprised and rather irritated by this off-handedness. I said, 'Oh, come on—getting this stuff out is the whole reason for coming here. So think about it a bit.'

'I don't mind. You decide,' and more than that I couldn't get out of her.

In the end I said, 'All right, then this is what we'll do —we'll give it two more days for appearances' sake, and then we'll take the car down to Malo Selo, pick up the stuff, probably putting the gold in the petrol tank of the car if we can't think of anything more original. Then we'll drive to Rijeka and go back the way we came.'

'All right,' she said indifferently.

That night we went to The National Theatre and saw a first-rate performance of *Hamlet*. It was in Serbo-Croat, of course, but with anything one knows as well as *Hamlet*, the language problem disappears. In fact, to hear it in a foreign language is almost an advantage, because you no longer have to listen for those lovely, almost too familiar words, and can watch the set of the actor's body and the movements of the players, and *see* the play as a universal masterpiece instead of just listening to it as a sort of recital. I enjoyed it immensely, and said so, and for once Katherina seemed pleased that I had liked something about contemporary Yugoslavia.

As we left the theatre she said, 'Look—I don't feel like going to bed yet. I've been told about a place where you can go and dance and have drinks and so on till quite late. How about trying it?'

'A night club?'

'I doubt if it s a night club in the sense that you mean. The Communists wouldn't approve of that. Night clubs are capitalist and decadent, so you mustn't expect the champagne-and-naked-girl sort of thing. But if you want a bit of night life, this is apparently quite fun.'

'Lead me to it.'

I have no idea where the place was, or what it was called, but it was a big room in a cellar, with a large number of brick pillars, which presumably held up the building above, and which made dancing rather tricky. The floor was polished wood, but it had been much worn, so that the knots in the wood stood up high above the general surface and were very painful to the feet. The walls were decorated with murals, in the best night club tradition. But as Katherina had said, the paintings were not of naked or semi-naked girls, but of boys and girls in Serbian national costume, dancing national dances. The whole effect, to a spoiled Westerner like myself, was a trifle grim, a trifle impoverished, but strangely moving. As we went in Katherina said, slightly anxiously, 'I warned you that this isn't a place for tourists. You're probably going to be bored sick.'

I said, 'My dear, I've been bored sick by every night club I've visited in the last twenty years. This at least has a style of its own.'

The place may or may not have been for tourists, but we were followed in by two blond German men, who were shown to a table next to ours. They may have been father and son, since one was in his early forties, and the other a boy of about twenty. The older one seemed to be distinctly drunk, and he gave his orders in that loud, domineering way which is the hallmark of Germans abroad, and then cursed the waiter, still in German, for some mistake which had been made in serving him. The place was very full, and I saw a number of heads turn in his direction as he rumbled and spluttered and gesticulated. I said to Katherina, 'What's the general attitude towards Germans here nowadays?'

She shrugged her shoulders and said, 'What would *your* attitude be if somebody had killed your mother and two of your cousins and then came here with a lot of money to spend?'

The band consisted of a man with a piano accordion, a man with a guitar and a violinist, and they played a curious mixture of things—half American pop music, and half traditional Serbian dances. Both seemed equally acceptable to the crowds which were now filling the place, and for myself, I just did what Katherina told me to do as best I could. So far all was peaceful. But after about the fourth dance we returned to our table and it was obvious that the older German was now even drunker and in the mood for trouble. He kept shouting loudly and angrily at the waiter and the floor manager, and occasionally threw in a few shouts at the world in general. I saw some ugly looks being cast at him, and I said to Katherina, 'I don't know what he's saying, but he sounds to me as though he's asking for trouble.'

'He is,' she said grimly. 'And if he isn't very careful, he'll get it. Most of these people are young Communists, and they don't like Germans anyway.'

The German was still bellowing away, and before I could stop her, Katherina turned and spoke sharply and contemptuously to him. What she said, I think, was that he was drunk and making a nuisance of himself. He snarled back at her, and made the gesture of spitting in her face, without actually doing any spitting, but nevertheless for a few minutes after that he subsided, and was comparatively silent, just going on drinking, and occasionally saying something to the younger man, who had been comparatively well behaved.

Meanwhile two young men came out, and one sang and the other danced—traditional Slav stuff with that curious business of the folded arms and bent knees, and feet flying out at the side. I don't think they were professionals, but just members of the audience, but they were quite good, and the audience obviously loved it. The whole thing was very simple and unsophisticated, but also very gay and charming. Katherina was obviously enjoying it, and so for that matter was I. But the older German had now had a couple more drinks, and he couldn't let it alone. When one of the young men began to sing another Serbian song, he suddenly began to roar out a song in German, in a vast, tuneless voice, and the younger man joined in. There were angry shouts from the audience, but he took no notice, and just went on roaring in his huge voice, thereby making a nonsense of the whole performance.

I must say that everybody was very patient with him, and when the singer had finished his song, and the other man had danced, they applauded loudly, as though nothing unusual was happening. But merely to be ignored did not suit the older German at all, so he simply picked up his glass and threw it on to the dance floor, so that it shattered and showered glass fragments all around. I saw the waiter and the floor manager hurrying across to him and said to Katherina, 'I think there's going to be a real rough-house in a moment, and I don't care for rough-houses. So let's pay and get out.'

But she said, 'Why? I want to see what happens.'

In any case we were too late. Our table was in the corner, and the Germans were next to us, and between us and the door. The floor manager, supported by the waiter, came over and spoke to them firmly, but entirely civilly. He was asking them to go. The older German leapt to his feet and screamed out something, which I was later told was to the effect that he had killed plenty of Yugoslavs in his time, and only wished he had killed more. With this he picked up a bottle from the table and swung it at the floor manager. The floor manager ducked, and the bottle hit the unfortunate waiter just on the collar bone. I think it broke it, for the man gave a scream of pain and staggered back clutching at his shoulder. That, at last, was too much, and in what seemed a couple of seconds the Germans' table, and therefore ours in the corner, was cut off by a crowd consisting of most of the men in the audience, roaring with fury. I jumped up, and shouted to Katherina, 'Get behind me!' and picked up my chair, which was the only weapon in sight. Somebody in the press to get at the Germans knocked our table over with a crash of breaking glass, and at that moment I heard another similar crash, and saw that the older German had broken the bottom off his bottle against another, and was holding it now with its jagged edges menacing the crowd which was pressing in on him. He was trapped in a corner, as we were behind him, but he was a big powerful man, and his table was still between him and the crowd, and he was flourishing the broken half of a bottle with its spiky glass, and just for a moment the crowd hesitated. We were, of course, half behind him, and I was just nerving myself to hit him with the chair, and realizing what a very awkward thing a chair is for such purposes, when a loud, authoritative voice shouted something in Serbo-Croat, and the crowd parted to let through a big man with startlingly brilliant blue eyes, whom I recognized as Petrov, the big young Serb whom Katherina and I had met in a restaurant some days previously. I did not know, and never shall know, whether he had been in the place some time, concealed from us by one of the pillars, or whether he had just come in. But it was obvious that most of the crowd knew him, and knew that he was somebody important. He spoke quietly, almost in an undertone, to the crowd, which drew back slightly, so that they were perhaps two or three yards from the table behind which the Germans were standing. Petrov walked forward until he was confronting them across the table—the older German still standing with his broken bottle poised. He spoke to them quietly in German and pointed to the door. He was obviously telling them to go while the going was good. But the older German was beyond all reason, and he suddenly let out a roar and leapt forward, overturning the table and stabbing desperately at Petrov's face with the broken bottle. I swung the chair to hit him, but before I could do so Petrov had knocked away the hand holding the broken bottle and had hit him neatly across the throat with the side of his hand, in the best traditions of unarmed combat, and in the way that looks so delightfully easy if you know how to do it. The man went down with a crash, and as he did so, I remembered that the sugar from the wrecked table poured down on his blond hair. The young German, who had been comparatively quiet until now, made a vicious kick at Petrov, but I had been expecting this, and caught him a hard prod in the back and body with the legs of my chair so that he staggered forward and tripped over the table, and then they were both down, and the mob had piled on top of them, and I saw a couple of flick knives flash out and thought they were dead. But Petrov called again in that loud authoritative voice, and they heard him, and slowly and reluctantly got up from the bodies of the two Germans. Then Petrov shouted an order, and immediately half a dozen men seized each of the Germans by his arms and legs and carried him to the door, and literally threw him into the street, amid a derisive yell from the crowd. People came streaming back to their tables, the band struck up, and everybody started to dance. The waiter with the broken collar bone had been led away, and apart from two overturned tables and a lot of mess on the floor in our corner, there was nothing to show that anything untoward had happened. I found that I was still holding the chair, and put it down rather sheepishly, as the floor manager and two waiters hurried across and started to clear up the mess. Petrov's voice at my elbow said, 'Good evening, Mr. Petersen. You and your wife are all right?'

I said, 'Quite all right, thank you. It just looked rather nasty for a moment.'

'Yes. I'm very sorry that it should have happened to you. This is usually a very well run, friendly place. But Germans have an uncanny knack of causing trouble amongst peaceful people.'

I said, 'You dealt with him beautifully.'

Petrov shrugged and said with his charming smile, 'It wasn't difficult. The man was so drunk that he could hardly stand anyhow. But I had to do something, otherwise I think he would probably have been killed. You must remember that a lot of these young people had parents or relatives killed by the Germans.'

I noticed, as I had noticed before in the restaurant, that though he was speaking to me, his eyes, as he said this, were on Katherina.

They were still cleaning up the mess, and Petrov said, 'Whilst they're cleaning up here, perhaps you would honour me by coming across to my table?'

We went across with him, and as we sat down Katherina said suddenly, 'You know I must confess that I rather enjoyed that.'

Petrov stared at her for a moment and then said, 'You enjoyed it, Mrs. Petersen? Why?'

'Because they were bullies, and I like seeing bullies put in their place—particularly if nobody gets killed, and they're just left looking fools.'

I said, 'The truth is, darling, that there was a nice hearty row, and you like rows. Personally, I am a man of peace.'

Petrov smiled at her and said, 'My sympathies are with Mrs. Petersen. I too, rather like rows—as long as they don't go too far.'

He insisted on buying us a drink, and a few moments later, when the band struck up with one of its rather odd versions of an out-of-date American tune, he said, 'Ah—this brings back memories.' He turned to me and said with great courtesy, 'Would it be in order if I were to ask Mrs. Petersen to dance with me?'

I said, 'Of course.'

They made an uncommonly handsome couple, and they were both good dancers, but looking back on the incident now, I remember noticing that, unlike most of the couples on the floor, they talked as they danced, and, for the most part, talked seriously and unsmilingly.

We stayed until after two o'clock in the morning, and as I remember it we ended with one of those Serbian round dances in which everybody takes part. Petrov tried very hard to pay our bill as well as his own, but I succeeded in preventing this. Our bill, by night club standards, was absurdly small anyhow. We parted eventually, very cordially, and as we walked to our hotel I said to Katherina, 'Well—I think you've made a conquest.'

'What do you mean? Conquest?'

'Petrov. He obviously has an eye to you.'

She said, 'Don't be ridiculous. He was only being polite.'

I said wearily, 'Sarah darling, I wish you wouldn't repeat yourself so. Don't you remember saying those

166

exact words to me, three years ago in New York, when you had spent the evening dancing with Matthew Gilder?'

There was a moment's silence and then she said, 'Do you mean you're jealous because I danced with another man?'

I said, 'Jealous? Of course not. I have no right to be jealous, whatever you do, have I? I'm only telling you, as a matter of interest, that that very handsome young man likes the look of you—which only shows his good taste.'

She made no reply to that and we walked back to the hotel in silence.

§

The following evening I had arranged to see Willie Strang, who was Second Secretary at the British Embassy, and practically my only acquaintance in Belgrade. I was to meet him at his apartment at six o'clock, and we were to have a drink and go out to dine together. Katherina had her usual date with the mysterious friends whom I was never allowed to meet, so it was agreed that we should just come back to the hotel separately after dinner.

Willie Strang was a strange character whom I had known at Cambridge. He had gone into the Diplomatic after the war, and had been a failed Diplomat ever since. A part of his failure might have been due to his appearance. He was at least six feet six in height and very thin. He wore steel rimmed spectacles and his long body was always bowed like a tree in a wind. He had a rather loud squawky voice, in which he talked with great rapidity, hardly ever finishing a sentence before beginning another. He took my hand in an excruciating bony grip and squawked out, 'Well, well, well—it's good to see you, Jim. It's been too . . . where have you come . . . are you staying long? What will you have? You must excuse . . . woman who does for me . . . with ice? . . . Well, how's everything been? . . . Hollywood eh? Must be a strange . . . I mean making films eh? Must be a strange life but very . . .'

During all this I had said nothing. I now said, 'Thank you, Willie. I would like a whisky and soda with no ice. Yes, I have been in Hollywood. It was very dull.'

He poured me out a drink and said, 'Dull, eh? Last thing one would have . . . I mean—lots of . . . here's your . . . Cheers my dear fellow . . .'

We drank to one another and Willie said, 'Do sit down, Jim. So nice . . . Well, here we are, eh?'

The conversation went on at this sort of level for some time, with Willie's characteristic imitation of a machine-gun firing rapid bursts, without ever quite contriving to say anything completely. But the apartment was comfortable and pleasant, and the drinks good, and above all, I was profoundly glad to have somebody to talk to. I realized that apart from Petrov, I had not spoken to anybody but Katherina for some days. Moreover, I knew that Willie was really by no means a fool, and that as he ceased to be shy he would become more coherent. I gathered that he liked Belgrade and the Yugoslavs, and in particular the Serbs, who he said were, 'A fine lot on the whole. Splendid chaps some of them. Don't give a damn for . . . I mean if they think something, out it comes . . . loud voice, and don't care who hears. . . . Informers . . . anybody.'

I said, 'What is the situation over that? I mean secret police and informers and so on? Before I came here I was told by some Yugoslavs in Paris that practically the whole population was in the pay of the police.'

'Bunkum,' said Willie firmly. 'There *are* secret police

of course. But if it comes to that where aren't there . . . ?
No more here than anywhere else and less than in some
places I've . . . After all, remember that you're in the
Balkans. Very political . . . everybody a politician. In
the towns that is. Now out in the country . . . No. A
peasant doesn't care whether the country's Communist
or Thursday. Doesn't make any difference to . . . things
just about the same for him as they always were. . . .
Better sometimes.'

'Is there much real poverty? I mean people starving
and that sort of thing?'

'Plenty of poverty. Always was. Not a rich . . . But
food all right on the whole. Lot of other things missing
because the country can't afford . . . Wages very low and
imported stuff very . . . Have to cut their . . . this last
devaluation . . . very hard on them. But it had to come.
Tried to go too fast you see. Refrigerators and cars and
so on. Raising the standard of life before the country
can afford it. Not an industrial country, and very few
natural resources. Not enough to export to pay for the
imports. Same problem as ours at home only more so.'

'Is the country on a whole solidly Communist?'

Willie waved a bony hand and said, 'Is no country as
a whole. About six countries. You've got Serbs, Croats,
Slovenes, Montenegrins and lord knows what else. And
all very proud of it. . . . Only one hundred per cent
Yugoslavs are the young Commies. As for being solid
Communist, it depends what you mean by . . . They're
not pro-West—or for us or America or anything like
that. Why should they be when they've got something
the size of Russia sitting on their back doorstep? But
they're not particularly pro-Russian either if it comes
to . . . They're just pro them. That's why they like the
Marshal. He's like them—he's just pro-Yugoslav.'

'They *do* like him?'

'Oh, lord yes. If it hadn't been for him they'd have been in somebody's pocket—Russia's or . . . long ago. It's only he who's kept them standing on their own. . . . The problem is what will happen when he dies? Most of the Cabinet's much more left than he is or than the country . . . a lot of people don't seem to realize it, but the Marshal's one of the most valuable lives in Europe.'

'What's the attitude of the Government towards opposition? Take all these émigrés that you find all over the world—in Paris and London and so on? Most of them are very anti-Communist.'

'I don't think the Government cares a damn about them nowadays. There's no really organized opposition movement. All those chaps can do is talk. And nobody listens. . . .'

'Some of them still take themselves very seriously.'

'Oh, sure. Slavs always take themselves seriously, if nobody else does. But most of these émigré chaps . . . twenty years out of date. Take that old chap who lives in Paris—what's his name?'

'Popovic?'

'That's right—the one who's blind. Well, he's been gone twenty years. Most Yugoslavs of thirty-five have never heard of . . . let alone the younger people.'

'What would happen, Willie, if one of these anti-Communist émigré chaps came back here and the police picked him up? Would he be liable to be shot or put in jug or what?'

'Oh, lord no. That's all over long ago. Nothing would happen to him, as long as he behaved himself and didn't cause . . . The Government's much more lenient now with people like that than it used to be. It can afford it. Take this chap Pelic that there's been all the fuss about. He's worse than any Royalist émigré. He's an ex-Communist turned anti. . . . Twenty years ago they'd have barely waited to find a convenient wall to put him up against. As it is, they don't even keep him in gaol.'

I said, 'I've never heard of Pelic.'

'Don't you read the papers?'

'I've been on the west coast of America, Willie, and the papers there give you all the news about local weddings and the Shriners' ball, but don't worry much about little things like Central Europe.'

'Well, Pelic is a rather interesting case. His father was one of the Marshal's right-hand men during the war and just after it. The son was only a kid then and he was sent to America and educated there. He became a very brilliant electrical engineer. Came back here about five years ago, just before his old man died—and was given a big government job, modernizing electrical . . . you know—controllers. . . . He was a Communist, of course, just as his father had been. But for some reason he got very bloody-minded about the whole thing, and very fed up about the way things were being run. . . . He's a Serb, and if Serbs don't like something, they can never keep their mouths shut. So Pelic wrote a book in which he said that the whole thing on the electrical side was a bloody mess, and couldn't compare with Western countries and never would as long as it was all mixed up with politics. As I say, it was a sort of book that would have got him shot in the old days, but all the Government did was to reprimand him and demand a withdrawal of . . . So on that he upped and wrote a series of articles, very ironical, withdrawing everything he had said and then saying it again louder. They had to do something about . . . so they shoved him in gaol for a few months and then let him out again. Of course they fired him from his job but apart from that, as far as I know he's a free man.'

At about seven-thirty Willie looked at his watch, and

said, 'Well, this has been very . . . old man. I wish we could have had longer together.'

I said, 'But aren't we dining?'

Willie looked aghast and said, 'My God—did I ask you to dine, Jim?'

'Well, yes—you did. But it doesn't matter if . . . ?'

'I seem to have put up a frightful black. I've got to be at the Embassy at eight. You'll just have to forgive me my . . . Terribly sorry. Peccavi and all that . . . but duty calls with strength like . . .'

I said, 'It doesn't matter in the least, Willie.'

§

That is why I happened to return to our hotel at about eight o'clock instead of at about eleven or twelve. That is why, also, I arrived in sight of the hotel just in time to see Katherina emerge from the entrance and set off down the street. I instinctively walked faster, to catch up with her and explain the change in my plans. And then suddenly I realized that I desperately wanted to know what it was that Katherina did on these evening expeditions, and I slowed down my pace and simply kept station some fifty yards behind her. She looked around several times, and I guessed that she was keeping a sharp eye out for Oliver Hardy in his bowler hat. But I was a far less impressive figure than Oliver Hardy, and I wasn't wearing a bowler hat, and she was not expecting to see me, so she simply walked on quickly and then turned down a side street, and by the time I got to the corner she had vanished. There was something familiar about the street, and I realized that it was the one in which there was the little restaurant we had been to before. I walked on down the street until I came to the restaurant, and stopped outside it. It was discreetly curtained, but there was a crack in the curtains and through that I could see the inside of the place. It was empty except for two people—Katherina and Petrov. They were sitting side-by-side on one of the banquettes laughing happily together, with the air of two people who are just settling down for an intimate dinner. And even as I looked, Petrov glanced round quickly to make sure that the waiters were occupied elsewhere, and then raised her hand and kissed it hard and passionately, looking, in doing so, more handsome than ever.

My first reaction, as far as I can remember, was one of mild indignation and jealousy, but not surprise. After all, I had known the night before, when they were dancing together in the night club, that Petrov was attracted by her, and had even told her so. The indignation, as it had been with Sarah and Matthew Gilder, was mainly due to the fact that she had not been frank with me—that something was going on behind my back. I had known instinctively for some days that Katherina was fencing behind the veil with me, but somehow I had thought that whatever was going on would be rather more serious than an affair with a handsome restaurant pick-up. I thought for a moment of just going into the restaurant and joining them, as the dumb Englishman who suspects nothing. But this would be awkward and probably unproductive, and since I could hardly go on standing outside the restaurant peeping through its windows, I turned away and made for the Moskva. At the corner where the side street met the main street, I nearly bumped into a big fat man who was wearing a bowler hat. We both muttered apologies and went on our ways—I to the Moskva and Oliver Hardy towards the restaurant.

Then I remembered two things. The first was that when we met Petrov on that first occasion he had spoken to her for a few moments in Serbo-Croat. As far as I was concerned, he might have said anything including, 'Meet me on Friday night at the Old Bull and Bush.' But if so, why should he think that she would understand Serbo-Croat when he had just been told that she didn't? The second thing I remembered was her face as he came into the restaurant that night. For one moment I had been sure that he was somebody she knew. That would fit together—that Petrov was really an old acquaintance —one of those shadowy 'friends' in Belgrade whom she sometimes referred to. But what was she doing with a friend of that kind in a place which she hadn't visited for twenty years? And why the solemn business of introducing himself as a complete stranger?

Then there was this matter of Oliver Hardy. I still found it difficult to believe that any secret police force would use Oliver as an agent, and even if they did I could not see how they could know who Katherina was, nor why they should be particularly interested in her. But the fact remained that Oliver and the bowler hat did tend to turn up all around us in a rather disconcerting way. I decided that the only thing to do was to tackle Katherina and force her to put her cards on the table, threatening to walk out on the whole business unless she did so. I was getting a little tired of complications.

It was nearly two hours before she arrived, and by that time I was beginning to realize that I had had no dinner, had drunk rather a lot of beer, and was not in a very good temper. She came over and sat down and said without greeting, 'That man's following me again.'

'Oliver?'

'The fat one with the bowler hat. I was having dinner with a friend, and when I came out he was hanging about outside and he followed me. There you are, you see—here he comes.'

Oliver came in and went across to his usual table and sat down with that air of the bored but faithful bulldog. I said, just to try it, 'With whom were you dining?'

'With Vodanic. He says that everything's arranged now, and he thinks we could go whenever we like.'

I said, 'If his name's Vodanic why does he call himself Petrov?'

That shook her. She looked up at me sharply and said in a low voice, 'What do you mean?'

I said rather irritably, 'Oh, come on, my dear—I know that you were dining with Jovan Petrov because I saw you in the restaurant together. So stop lying and trying to be clever and tell me what really goes on, or else I quit.'

'What do you mean by that?'

'I mean that I shall simply pack up, take the passports with me and go, and leave you to sort out your own muddles. I'm sick of all this back-stairs business.'

She said rather breathlessly, 'You wouldn't do that, Jim—not leave me alone. . . .'

'I certainly would if I have any more of this double-crossing stuff. I've played rather more than fair with you about this whole expedition, and if you can't play fair with me I want no further part in you.'

There was a long pause and then she said quietly, 'All right. What do you want to know?'

'Why were you having dinner with Petrov this evening?'

'Why shouldn't I have dinner with a friend of mine?'

'How long has he been a friend of yours?'

'You were there when I met him.'

'But that wasn't the first time you'd met him, was it?'

She hesitated and I said, 'Come on now, don't fence. You knew him before, didn't you?'

She saw that the game was up and said dully, 'Yes.'

'How long have you really known him?'

'I met him five years ago in Paris.'

'Then why did you pretend, and why did *he* pretend, that you'd never met before?'

'We just thought it better . . . that you shouldn't know,' she said rather helplessly.

'Because you thought I should be jealous?'

'Yes.'

I said bitterly, 'You flatter yourself, my dear. Why should I care how many handsome friends you have? What was he doing in Paris anyhow?'

'He was on his way home from America. He was in Paris for a couple of weeks and . . .' She shrugged her shoulders, 'There you are.'

'You fell in love with him?'

'I . . . don't know . . . I suppose I did, in a way. I was very lonely, and he was very charming to me. Then he went to Belgrade, but we wrote to each other. So when we came here, I arranged to meet him.'

'Well, what was there in that to make a mystery about? You meet a young Serb in Paris, and you come to Belgrade, and he's in Belgrade and you want to see him. What's wrong with that? If you'd told me, of course I should have understood. We didn't need all this play-acting nonsense about your being strangers and so on.'

She hesitated for a moment and then said quietly, 'There's rather more to it than that, Jim.'

'Well, then, for God's sake out with it.'

'Well, first of all his name isn't Petrov. His name is Pelic. Does that mean anything to you?'

I said, 'It wouldn't have, until this evening. But I've been talking to Willie Strang at the Embassy, and now it means quite a lot. He's the man who's been having a row with the Government?'

'Yes . . .' she hesitated and then said in a low voice, 'He gave up everything to come back. He had a wonderful job in America, and then his father wrote to him and said that the country needed him, and so he . . . came back. That was when I met him in Paris. He was on his way back, and full of it—how it was the duty of every young Yugoslav to come home and help the Government. He was cross with me because I didn't want to come. And then he got back here, and it was all right for a bit, and then he began to see how rotten it all was . . . and because he's a person who has to tell the truth he said so. And then they . . . threw him out of his job, and put him in prison and . . .' Her voice broke and she took her face in her hands.

I said, 'Well, as I understand it, as Communists' Governments go, this one's treated him very leniently.'

'Oh, yes,' she said dully. 'They haven't killed him, if that's what you mean. But what is he to do now? I tell you he gave up everything to come here. And now they won't let him out of the country, and won't let him work, and spy on him all the time, and . . .'

I said, 'Ah—now this at last begins to make some sense. If you've been spending time with Pelic I can well see that you might have a man with a bowler hat keeping an eye on you. I couldn't imagine the police being interested in you, but I can quite see that they might be interested in *him*. I think you'll find that in the official records, as reported by our friend Hardy over there, you'll appear as Sarah Petersen, an English woman who has met and fallen for Pelic and is having an affair with him.'

She said nothing, but just sat staring blankly at the table, so I said, 'Are you in love with him now?'

She said irritably, 'I wish you wouldn't keep asking me about being in love with him. I tell you I don't

177

know. Anyhow, if I did, what would be the use of being in love with somebody you can't have?'

She stared down at the table again and said drearily, 'It's all so hopeless. In a couple of days' time we shall be gone, and then I shall be back in Paris and he'll be in Belgrade. I can't come to him and he can't come to me. What's the use of that to either of us?'

I said, 'If you're really in love with him, why shouldn't you just stay here and marry him, and damn the consequences? Tell the authorities who you really are, and say you want to stay here. From what Willie Strang told me this evening they probably wouldn't do anything about it anyhow.'

Katherina shook her head irritably and said, 'Don't be absurd. Of course they wouldn't let me stay, even if I wanted to, which I don't. I may or may not be in love, but I'm certainly not in love enough to be willing to live in a Communist country. Anyhow, Jovan would never marry me as things are at the moment. I tell you it's all quite . . . hopeless.'

'Then what do you propose to do about it?' She raised her eyes just for a moment and looked at me and then lowered them again. 'Go away,' she said dully. 'Go away and forget the whole silly business. What else can I do? I ought never to have let it happen anyway.'

I said, 'You're sure that that's what you really want—to be out of it?'

'Of course it is. Can't you see that being here, like this, is just hell?'

She said it rather huskily and I saw that her eyes were full of tears. I said, 'All right—if you're sure that's what you really want. It's just like the time when you fell for Matthew Gilder and then wished you hadn't, and I had to get you out of New York and take you to the west coast. Except that this time, instead of taking you to the west coast, your devoted husband, James Petersen, has got to get you back to Paris as soon as he can.'

Katherina gave a sort of moan and said, 'Oh, yes —yes! Get me out, Jim. For God's sake get me out.'

I said, 'All right then—you say there's no reason why we shouldn't go now, so let's go.' I thought for a moment or two and then said, 'This is what we'll do—we'll tell them at the hotel that we're going touring for a few days and are coming back. We'll pay the bill up to date and leave a suitcase behind to reserve our room to make it all look probable. To-morrow night we'll drive to the village, pick up the stuff from your grandparents and make for Rijeka. And then, as long as we can get the stuff through the customs, you'll be in Italy and be able to breathe again.'

She said, 'That would be marvellous.' She sighed and added, 'I don't know what sort of mess I should have made of this without you, Jim.' She squeezed my hand hard, and I lifted her hand and kissed it lightly and looked across to see if this had registered with Hardy. But Oliver was already waddling towards the door, his stint of duty done.

I said, 'How about Pelic. What is he expecting you to do now?'

'Oh, he knows that we may go at any time. We agreed this evening that there was nothing to be done about it, and more or less said good-bye.'

'So you don't need to see him again?'

She closed her eyes and sat for a moment or two in silence and then said, with her eyes still closed, 'What I need is to be back in Paris, with some money. I know you say it won't be much, but to be back in Paris with even a little bit of money would be heaven.'

13

THE following morning as we were breakfasting, Katherina said, 'There's one person that I must see before we go, and that's Vodanic. He's been very good to me and I must see him to say thank you.'

I said, 'Can't you telephone him?' I was anxious not to let her out of my sight now, in case there was any more funny business.

'You can't talk on the telephone here. The lines are certain to be tapped.'

'But that doesn't matter if you're only going to say good-bye. It just confirms what we've already told the hotel.'

Katherina hesitated and then said rather reluctantly, 'All right. Then I'll go down and telephone now.'

She came back about ten minutes later and said, 'It's just as well I did talk to him. The stuff's been moved out of the old people's place for safety.'

'Then where is it now?'

'In another house on the outskirts of the village. An old friend of my grandfather's is looking after it.'

'And he'll be prepared to hand over to us?'

'Oh, yes. He'll have been warned that we're coming.'

'Will you be able to find the place in the dark?'

'I think so. It's just this side of the village and stands by itself.'

We set off just after dark. I had brought the car round, and as we loaded up the luggage, I happened to notice a very fine big Mercedes parked just behind us. There were few cars of that kind about in Belgrade, and it occurred to me that this one could very easily be a police car. We started off, and after we had gone a short distance I glanced in the mirror, and sure enough the Mercedes was just moving away from the hotel behind us. I said nothing to Katherina. She was tense and nervous enough already, without any false alarms. But when we had gone a mile or so and the Mercedes was still behind, I pulled up under some pretext of fastening a bonnet catch, in order to see what would happen. The Mercedes drove straight by, travelling fast, and vanished round the corner. I just had time to see that there were two men in it, but neither of them was wearing a bowler hat. I glanced in the mirror occasionally over the next few miles but there was never any sign of the Mercedes.

It took us about twenty minutes to reach the outskirts of the village. Katherina said, 'Go slowly now. It's somewhere close here . . . That's right—just where that patch of trees is.'

The house stood well back from the road among the trees, approached by what had once been a drive, but was now thickly covered with grass and moss. As I swung the car round the drive, my headlights lit up the house for a moment, and I saw that it was a medium-sized, dilapidated-looking place, and caught a glimpse of a couple of broken windows. As we pulled up I said, 'This doesn't look to me a very safe place to keep anything. I should have thought the stuff would have been safer in the grand piano.'

Katherina said, 'Nobody lives here now, because it's going to be knocked down. That was why it was such a good hiding place, because nobody would think of looking here for anything valuable.'

'Is there anybody here? It doesn't look much like it.'

'You'll see in a minute. Switch your lights off.'

I said, 'Wait a minute—I've got a torch.'

By the light of the torch we went up the steps to the front door, which looked as though it hadn't been painted for many years. Katherina said in a low voice, 'It won't be locked.' She went forward and pushed the door and it creaked open. The place was in complete darkness, but Katherina went boldly in, and I was following with the torch when suddenly I heard the sound of a car on the road outside, and glancing over my shoulder, saw headlights through the trees, coming fast down the road from Belgrade. They were very big bright lights, and I knew instinctively that it was the Mercedes. I turned and started to say, 'I believe there's . . .' when the torch was wrenched violently from my hand and simultaneously the door banged shut behind me.

A voice said, 'Lights!'

A single naked electric bulb went on, and by it I saw the Petrov-Pelic character. He was wearing a trilby hat and a raincoat, which made him look faintly like an American gangster. To support the idea, he was holding a large Luger automatic, which was pointed at my stomach. He said politely, 'Will you please raise your hands, Mr. Petersen?'

I looked from one to the other of them. Katherina was still standing by the light switch. She was deathly pale. I said, 'Now what on earth is this all about? More funny business?'

Pelic said sharply, 'Never mind about that. Raise your hands. If you don't I shall have to kill you, which I shouldn't like to do.' The Luger looked businesslike and so did he, so I put my hands up. He said, 'Now, please sit down here,' and pointed to a heavy wooden chair—the only article of furniture in the room. I sat down, and he ran his hands rather perfunctorily over

182

me, at the same time saying to Katherina, 'He doesn't carry a gun?'

She shook her head in silence. Pelic said, 'Good. Where are the passports, Mr. Petersen?'

I began to see light. I said, 'Katherina has hers. Mine is in my right-hand overcoat pocket.'

He put the Luger against my chest and felt for the passport and pulled it out. He said, 'Thank you,' and stepped back a couple of paces still carefully keeping me covered. 'Well now, Mr. Petersen, I'm afraid I shall have to borrow this for a few days. I give you my word that it shall be returned to you when we have finished with it. I shall also have to borrow your car.'

I said, 'I think I get the idea. You're going to make a dash for it on my passport, eh?'

'Yes. That's right. I'm sorry, but I have no alternative.'

I said, 'You realize that it'll take you at least twenty-four hours to get across the border, and in that twenty-four hours every way out of the country will have been alerted?'

'Oh, yes,' said Pelic calmly. 'We have thought of that. It is the reason why it is so important that you should not be in a position to raise the alarm. By far the simplest way, of course, would be to kill you. This is a deserted place and it would certainly be some days before your body was found. But Katherina strongly objects to the idea of killing you.'

I looked at Katherina and said sarcastically, 'I'm extremely obliged to her.'

She was staring at me with the big eyes and the pale face on which her make-up stood out almost grotesquely. She said nothing. Pelic said, 'So I shan't kill you unless you make it absolutely necessary. I shall just . . . immobilize you so that you can't go rushing off to the nearest telephone.' He put his hand into his pocket and pulled out a big roll of surgical tape. He said, 'Katherina . . .' She came slowly across the room and took the gun. They fumbled the changeover slightly, and during that moment nobody was covering me, and I wondered whether to dive forward and try and knock it out of their hands and crack Pelic one in the way that a film hero would have done. But I am too old and soft for that sort of thing nowadays, and I had seen enough the previous night to tell me that he was pretty good at unarmed combat, so I let the moment of opportunity pass. Pelic unrolled some of the surgical tape and started to take my wrist to the arm of the chair. I thought of the Mercedes sitting outside there waiting, and I could not help smiling. Pelic noticed the smile and said, 'I am glad you are taking this so good temperedly, Mr. Petersen.'

I said, 'And how long am I supposed to stay here? Till I starve?'

'Oh, no—that is all organized. In forty-eight hours' time the police will be informed that you are here. I'm afraid that forty-eight hours will be rather uncomfortable, but at least it's better than being shot.'

The big Luger was wavering as Katherina's hand trembled. She put her other hand under the barrel to steady it. I said, 'I *am* going to be shot if we're not all very careful. Katherina doesn't look at all safe with that.' I said to her gently, 'Put that silly gun down, darling, before you do somebody some harm.'

She hesitated for a long moment and then suddenly she let the automatic drop to her side and put a hand over her eyes. Pelic looked up and saw that she was no longer covering me and said sharply, 'Katherina! . . .' but she only gave a groan and muttered something which sounded like 'Help me . . . help me!'

I said, 'All right. I would have helped you in the first

place if you had trusted me, instead of all this gun-waving nonsense.'

Pelic had already strapped one of my wrists to the arm of the chair, but I leant across and ripped the tape off with my other hand and said, 'Now let's see what we can do to save your silly necks.'

Pelic turned on Katherina and said bitterly, 'You'll ruin everything. Give me that gun.'

She turned away from him and muttered, 'No, Jovan. No . . . I can't do it.'

I said, 'It's just as well for you you can't, because I'm the only person who still might be able to save you both.'

Pelic wheeled sharply and said, 'What do you mean?'

'What I mean is that the police are sitting outside this house waiting for you now. If you go outside that door you'll walk straight into them.'

He hesitated and then said without conviction, 'I don't believe it.'

'Very well then—just carry on with your fine plan and see what happens. Or else do as I tell you, which at least gives you an outside chance.'

He said, 'What makes you think the police are here? Did you bring them?'

'No. They followed us from the hotel. I lost them on the road, but then they turned up again just as we came in and you jumped me.'

I turned to Katherina and said, 'Before I agree to help you, I want the answer to one question—was getting him out the real reason for your getting me to bring you here?'

She said almost in a whisper, 'Yes.'

'So right from the start you were double-crossing me, and all that business about the gold and the jewellery was just a front for what you were really up to?'

She shook her head in protest and said, 'No. That was

185

quite genuine. The stuff is here—in this house. We were going to take it with us.'

I said in some disgust, 'Well, after all that I'm surprised that you objected to something as simple as just having me shot.'

She said, very low, 'I'm sorry.'

I said, 'Don't apologize, my dear. After all, why should I be anything to you? You're not my wife Sarah, and never were, and never could be, and never have been for one moment in this whole farce.'

She looked at me with her eyes full of tears and her lips moved, but no sound came out. I turned to Pelic and said, 'Well now, let's get on with the business. The only chance is to draw those fellows outside off you. It's you they're really interested in, not Katherina, and if they think they see you making a bolt for it, they'll probably follow. We're about the same size, and in the dark they may not be able to tell us apart, so give me your hat and raincoat.'

He took off his hat and raincoat and handed them to me in silence. I put them on and they fitted very well. I turned up the collar of the raincoat and pulled the hat down as far as it would go. I took out my wallet and said, 'Here you are—here are two open vouchers for the journey from Belgrade to Paris on the Simplon. The Simplon stops at the village station here and it comes through some time soon. The passports you've got already. I shouldn't think you can take the gold—it's too heavy. But you might be able to take some of the jewellery. Now this is what you do—I shall make a dash for the car and drive off as fast as I can. You wait to see if they follow me. If they don't we're sunk and I can't do any more for you. But if they do follow, wait a moment or two and then leg it down to the village station as fast as you can and try and get on the Simplon.

If you manage it, you'll be in Zagreb to-morrow morning and across the border to-morrow afternoon. Got it?'

Pelic nodded and said, 'Yes.'

I said, 'Good-bye, my children, and good luck.'

I was turning to the door when Katherina suddenly ran forward and threw her arms round my neck. She was sobbing. She said chokily, 'Jim . . . Jim . . .'

I kissed her and then gently undid her arms from round my neck and said, 'No, darling—joke over now. But what I said wasn't quite true—there were just a few moments when you might almost have been Sarah. Put the light out.'

Pelic put the light out and I went to the door and opened it just a crack and looked out. Everything outside was very dark, and still and silent. I could see the outlines of the Alfa, but there was no sign of the Mercedes, and I guessed that, if it was there at all, it was parked among the trees. That meant that in order to head back for Belgrade, I should have to go past them. That didn't matter. It was important that they should see enough of me to think that I was Pelic.

I flung the door open with loud creakings, and dashed across the drive to the Alfa. The thought struck me with wry humour that it was all rather like a driver running to his car at the start of the Le Mans race. The engine fired at once, and I went off with a fine Italian roar of engine, and spinning back wheels, and swung out on to the road by which we had come. There was a long straight directly ahead of me, and on it I put my foot hard down for the first time since I had had the car, and was pleased to see that she ran up very quickly to something near a hundred and forty kilometres an hour, which is getting on for ninety. I had no doubt that the big Mercedes would be faster than that, but on a road that was mainly twisty, the little car might be just as

187

fast as the big one. The straight must have been a mile long, and I was three-quarters of the way down it, going all out, but with no sign of anything behind me. I was just beginning to think that I might have got it all wrong and that the Mercedes and the police might not be there at all. If they weren't, so much the better. I had got myself out of a nasty spot, and given Pelic and Katherina a reasonable chance of getting away. But at that moment I saw big headlights swing into the road at the far end of the straight, and I knew the chase was on. With the wind whipping my face in the open car, I wriggled down as comfortably as I could into the driving seat and decided to give them a run for it.

After the long straight the road went into its normal series of curves, and I swore to myself as I realized that whereas I had only driven back to Belgrade on one previous occasion, the driver of the Mercedes almost certainly knew the road like the back of his hand. But the Alfa's headlights and brakes were excellent, and she held the road like stamp-paper. With judicious use of the gear-box, and with no oncoming traffic, so that one could choose one's line on the corners, I could keep moving as fast as anything could do on a road like that. It was only ten miles to Belgrade, and I had had nearly a mile start. Once in the city, it would be comparatively easy to shake them off. I decided, as I threw the Alfa in and out of the bends, that I was probably going to get away with it.

Only a few moments later, I was not so sure. Through the bends I could not see the Mercedes' lights behind me, or estimate how far away it was. But now we came to another long straight and here the lights behind me shone up in my mirror rather disconcertingly early. The Mercedes was undoubtedly closing me, fast as I was driving. We had already covered nearly half the distance

188

to Belgrade, and I still doubted if they could catch me before we got there. But the way things were going it began to look as though we should arrive in the city with the Mercedes right on my tail, which might be awkward. Somehow I had to go faster, so I got lower in my seat to reduce the windage, and began to leave my braking for the corners later and later.

I think to this day that I might have got away with it if I had not allowed myself to be hustled in this way, but as it was I twice noticed a slight tendency for the back end of the car to break away, and then I went into what looked, in my headlights, to be an innocent right-hander, and only realized a fraction of a second too late that it was one of those corners which goes on going round for longer than you think it is going to. I braked hard, and still might have got round, but the road surface was loose gravel and the back wheels lost their grip, the back end broke away, and the car spun. I think she spun three times like a top, and then, completely out of control, dived off the road, still at high speed, into some bushes. I remember thinking as she was spinning, 'You're dead.' Then there was a tremendous jar and I felt myself flying through the air.

I lay for a moment half stunned and then staggered to my feet and fought my way out of the bushes that had broken my fall. Very gingerly I tried my arms and legs, but they all seemed to be working, and the only damage I seemed to have suffered was that my face was badly scratched by the bushes. I looked round dazedly for the car, but there was no sign of it in the darkness, and everything was very still and silent, except for the distant sound of an approaching car. Then I remembered the Mercedes, and was only just in time to throw myself down among the bushes as it came tearing round the corner with blazing lights, and shot away on the Belgrade road with a fine whine of acceleration. Only when the sound of its engine had died away did I start to look for my car. I still could not see it, but I found a gap in the bushes where something had torn through them, and decided that this is where we must have gone off the road. I followed this torn-up track, groping and cursing the fact that I had no torch, and then suddenly found that I was standing on the very edge of a sheer drop. I could not tell, in the darkness, how deep a drop it was, but there was no doubt that somewhere at the bottom of it lay my gallant Alfa. It had torn through the bushes and gone over the edge, and had I not been thrown out I should have gone over the edge with it.

I was still feeling rather dazed, so I sat down and lit a cigarette and tried to think slowly and carefully. Clearly there was no point in going to look for the Alfa in the dark, over what might easily be a drop of a hundred feet. She was probably smashed to pieces, and even if she wasn't, and by some miracle in running order, there was no possible means of getting her back on to the road. The Alfa was clearly a write-off. So here I was some four or five miles from Belgrade with nothing whatever but the clothes I stood up in. I must have sat there for half an hour considering this, still rather slowly and laboriously, and at the end of that time I could think of nothing better than to start to walk into Belgrade.

I set off and walked for about two miles. The only satisfactory feature of the whole business was that during this walk I saw nothing of the Mercedes. I certainly seemed to have shaken it off, though it had been rather an expensive way of doing so. During the whole of this two miles, only two cars passed me coming from Belgrade, and each time as I saw their headlights I dodged into the projecting shrubs. But neither was the Mercedes, so I plodded on. Then at last something came from the other direction—a big lorry grinding along noisily and rather slowly. I dashed out into the road and flagged it down. It ground even more, and came to a halt, and I went up to the driver's cabin and jerked my thumb and said, 'Belgrade?' I saw that he was hesitating, so I pulled out my wallet and produced a five thousand dinar note and held it up. That was conclusive and he opened the door of the cabin and I got in.

We did not talk on the journey. We couldn't. I tried English, French and Italian but got no response to any of them. He tried Serbo-Croat, and German and got little response from me, since the only German I know is the German of Lieder, and somehow 'Ich grolle nicht' or 'Stille nacht' hardly seemed to be appropriate. Apart from that my only success was when I remembered the German for 'smoke' and said 'rauch?' and handed him a cigarette. After that we smoked in a rather uncomfortable silence until we reached Belgrade. I gave him his five thousand dinars and said 'Thank you and good luck' in every language I could manage, and we parted.

It is here that I made a stupid but, in the circumstances, perhaps pardonable mistake. I had never had time to work out exactly what I was going to do if I succeeded in shaking off the Mercedes and getting back to Belgrade, and now, still shaken up and perhaps mildly concussed by the crash I was incapable of working out anything. My passport had gone with Pelic and Katherina, and my luggage had gone over the edge with the Alfa. No hotel was likely to take me in these circumstances, even though I still had plenty of money. All I could think of was to head for what had been our hotel, where at least they knew me, and still had a suit-case of ours.

Accordingly I made for the hotel, where they looked at me rather strangely, as well they might, for I had lost

Pelic's hat in the crash, and was still wearing his rain-coat, which was torn in several places, and my face was covered in scratches from the bushes. But they accepted without comment my story that there had been a change of plan and that I wanted to use the room we had reserved.

I went up to the bedroom and washed the blood off my face. The suit-case we had left behind as a pledge of our return was still there, and I hoped for one moment that it might contain something useful. But all it *did* contain was Katherina's famous pink flannelette school-girl pyjamas, which were no real help in my present circumstances. As I put the pink pyjamas back in the suit-case I remembered with something of a pang how charming Katherina had looked in them on that first night in Paris. It was still only about eleven o'clock, but with any luck she and Pelic would now be on their way to Zagreb, and in just over twelve hours they would be clear.

Then suddenly the significance of those twelve hours hit me. I had left Belgrade with a wife, a car and my passport. Here I was back in Belgrade without any of them, and in the meantime the police would have lost touch with Pelic. It would need no particular brilliance on their part to put two and two together and decide that my return and the loss of my passport, and the disappearance of Pelic and Katherina, were connected. Even supposing my plans had worked, and that Pelic and Katherina had caught the train, it would still be perfectly simple for the authorities to have them picked up at Zagreb, or when they tried to cross into Italy. It was essential to leave the police in the dark as to who was where for at least another twelve hours.

I cursed myself now for ever having come back to the hotel. For if Katherina's views of the doings of hotels in

192

Belgrade were in any way to be trusted, my return would certainly be reported to the police, if only as a matter of routine: and the one thing I did not want was for the police to be able to question me for the next twelve hours. There was nothing for it but to get out of the hotel and somehow contrive to lose myself in Belgrade until the danger point was past.

Accordingly, I went down and out of the front door with a purposeful air, though in fact I had no idea where I was going. When I had gone about fifty yards, I went and stood in the shadow of a doorway, within sight of the hotel entrance. I gave it several minutes, but nobody came out, so I thought it safe to assume that I was not being followed. It would be dangerous, as well as useless, to go to another hotel with no luggage and no passport, so after a few moments hesitation I decided that the only thing to do was to sleep rough, and made for the Kalimegdan Gardens. Near them I found a public seat which overlooked the Danube, and I went and sat on it, for all the world like a homeless man sitting on the Thames Embankment. I was very tired, but not at all sleepy, and I sat there for several hours working out what my eventual story should be.

The clocks had struck four some time ago when I finally hit on the story of the Injured Husband. This amounted to telling as much of the truth as I possibly could—how I had discovered that my wife was having an affair with a man named Petrov, whom we had met casually; how I had decided to take her away, and how on some pretext she had lured me to the empty house. Once there, I had been suddenly confronted by Petrov with a pistol and my passport had been taken from me at pistol point. I had realized that I was going to be killed, and making a dash for it, had got away in the car with the intention of telephoning the police. Why had I not telephoned the police? Because on the way back to Belgrade I had had an accident and my car had been destroyed. Witness the scratches and bruises on my face, and the remains of the car if they liked to go and find them. I had lain all night unconscious and then in the morning had staggered back to Belgrade on foot and telephoned the British Embassy for help (as by that time I should have done—witness, Willie Strang).

There was one big snag even in this story—the fact that I had been to that wretched hotel. But I was too tired by now to try to polish the story any further, and my last waking thought was that at least checking up on my story would take a nice long time—long enough for it to be sure that Katherina and Pelic were safe. What happened after that, or what they did to me, didn't really matter much. I had nothing to lose.

14

AFTER that I went to sleep, and despite the hardness of the seat, slept until after nine o'clock, when I awoke feeling very stiff and sore. There were still two or three hours to go before it would be safe for me to make any move, so I went into the gardens until midday, and then went down to the Moskva, ate some croissants and drank some coffee, and then went and telephoned Willie at the Embassy.

I said, 'Willie, this is Jim. Jim Petersen. Look—I want your help. I've lost my passport.'

'Lost your . . . ?' Willie machine-gunned back. 'That's very awkward. Very . . . How did you manage it?'

'It's a long story. I'll tell you when I see you. In the meantime, will you be able to issue me another?'

'Well, yes. Probably. Eventually. But it's a hell of a long . . . very tedious . . . lot of red tape to be gone . . . Have you reported it to the police?'

'Not yet. You see I don't speak Serbo-Croat, so it's a bit difficult for me to try to explain anything like that on the telephone. I thought it might be best if I were to come and see you.'

'Sure,' said Willie. 'Come right along and we'll see what we can . . .'

I said, 'I'll be with you in a few minutes.'

As it turned out, however, this was an underestimate of the time before I was to see Willie Strang again, for as I came out of the telephone box I saw the big Mercedes draw up outside the door and thought, 'Here it comes.' I glanced at my watch. It was half past twelve. For some ridiculous reason I suddenly remembered again those pink flannelette pyjamas of Katherina's, and what she had looked like when she climbed up the ladder into the top berth of the sleeper, and a great wave of relief and happiness swept over me. With any luck, she was all right by now, and nothing mattered any more.

As I reached the door two men got out of the Mercedes. They were a sort of Mutt and Jeff act—a tall rather thin-faced man who looked as though he might suffer from dyspepsia, and a short, red-faced, rather jolly-looking man. They were both in plain clothes. They approached me and the tall man gave a sort of half bow and said politely in quite good English, 'Police please. Your name?'

'Petersen. James Petersen.'

'You are British?'

'Yes.'

'May I kindly see your passport?'

I said, 'I haven't it with me.' I was still playing for time and wanted the conversation to go on as long as possible.

The tall man said, 'Your passport is at your hotel?'

'No—I've lost it.'

'You have lost it,' said the tall man sadly. 'That is unfortunate.' He motioned towards the Mercedes and said, 'You will now please come with us.'

'What for?' I said with surprise, to make it a bit longer.

'It is desired to ask you some questions.'

'What about?'

He shrugged and said, 'You will hear the questions later. In here please.' He opened the back door of the Mercedes and I got in. He got in beside me and the cheerful little man with the red face took the wheel. I reflected that if he was the man who had been driving the previous night, then he was certainly a very good driver indeed.

§

The man who was sitting at the desk was small and slight, with thinning hair and spectacles. I should think he was about fifty. He had a lean, pointed face, and in most respects he looked like one's idea of the typical civil servant. The most striking thing about him, however, was his mouth, which was practically lipless. When he spoke he showed his teeth, several of which were made of something which looked like stainless steel. He and the tall man spoke in Serbo-Croat for a few moments, and then the tall man bowed and went out. The man at the desk said, 'You are Mr. Petersen?'

'Yes.'

'Markovic. Captain Markovic. Please sit down.' His English was perfect, without a trace of accent.

I sat down opposite him, noting with inward amusement that the room was so arranged that the person being interviewed had the light, which was very strong, full on his face, while Markovic's face was in the shadow. He said, 'I understand that you cannot produce your passport?'

'No.'

'It is a very serious matter for a foreign visitor to be here with no passport. How did you come to lose yours?'

'It was stolen from me.'

'Stolen?' he said sharply, showing the steel teeth in a curious sort of half grin with no mirth in it. 'In what circumstances?'

I began, 'Well—it's a long story . . .' but he suddenly held up his hand and said:

197

'One moment . . . Can you first tell me where you spent last night?'

This was the one question that I had wanted to avoid, and it came so unexpectedly that I had to hesitate for a moment to be sure that I was remembering correctly what I had finally decided should be the story. I said, 'I spent last night, or most of it, lying unconscious in some bushes about five miles out of Belgrade.'

He repeated, 'Lying in some bushes five miles out of Belgrade?'

He said it rather in the manner of the "feed" man of a pair of comedians, who repeats the question so as to allow the comedian to make a joke.

I said, 'Yes—that's part of the story about my passport. You see . . .'

He held up his hand again and said, 'One moment—have you reported the loss of your passport?'

'Yes—I've reported it to the British Embassy to Mr. William Strang, the Second Secretary.'

'And to the police?'

'No. I don't speak Serbo-Croat, and I find telephoning difficult, so I thought I would leave it to the Embassy to deal with the whole matter.'

'Please go on.'

'Well, you see, my wife and I were here on holiday . . .'

Once again the hand went up. Markovic said, 'One moment. Where is your wife now?'

I was finding this dodging about very disconcerting, and it was on the tip of my tongue to say that my wife had received an urgent message to return to Paris and that I had been to see her off. I only remembered just in time that this was part of a previous story which I had thought of and discarded. I said bitterly, 'I don't know. I wish I did.'

'You don't know, you wish you did?' he said, doing the comedian's feed stuff again.

'Yes. That's a part of the story too. My wife and I were on holiday here and one night in a restaurant, a man came up and introduced himself to us as Jovan Petrov.'

'Jovan Petrov.'

'Yes. He spoke English very well, but with an American accent.'

'With an American accent. And then . . . ?'

I hesitated, as a man might when coming to a delicate matter and said, 'Well, then later I found out that my wife was having an affair with Petrov, so I decided to get her out of Belgrade. . . .'

Up went the hand. 'One moment. *How* did you discover that she was having an affair with Petrov?'

'I followed her one night and saw them together.'

'And you decided to get her out of Belgrade?'

'Yes. So we started off last night . . .'

I went on and gave him the 'Injured Husband' story. This time he let me go on, only putting in an occasional question. I must say that told in cold blood to somebody else the story seemed even thinner than I had thought it would—particularly those parts of it which were entirely true, like the business of being threatened with an automatic. Here he put in one of his comparatively rare questions, to ask me if I saw what sort of automatic it was. I said, 'A Luger.'

'A Luger. Please go on?'

When I came to the end of the story we sat for a long time in silence and then Markovic said, 'And at what time did you arrive in Belgrade this morning?'

'I'm not absolutely sure. I should think it's about five miles from where the crash happened, and I remember that when I regained consciousness I looked at my watch and it was about nine o'clock. But I was very badly shaken up and bruised and I could only just walk at all. I should guess that I got back here at somewhere round about half past eleven.'

'And then you telephoned the Embassy?'

'Yes. I had only just finished telephoning them when your men picked me up.'

'Quite.'

He ruminated for a few moments, staring down at his blotter, then he looked up and said, 'Well, it is an interesting story, Mr. Petersen, and in many ways a very sad one. You seem to have been shamefully treated by . . . your wife and this man . . . Petrov.' He was staring at me very closely as he said it, and the steel teeth were very prominent. He said, 'Is there anything else you have to tell me?'

'I don't think so.'

'Very well, then—I don't think we can get any further at the moment. I shall have to ask you to stay with us for a short while, but we will make you as comfortable as we can.'

'You mean you're going to detain me?'

'There is no need to put it like that. It is just that we may need your co-operation again. There are certain inquiries which have not yet been completed.' He rang a bell, and a uniformed policeman entered.

I said, 'May I telephone the British Embassy?'

'That may be possible later. Good-bye for the present, Mr. Petersen. We shall probably meet again later.'

They took me downstairs to the basement, to a small room which was a sort of mixture of a cell and a bed-sitting-room. It had no window, but was lit by a neon strip. The floor and the walls were of unfaced concrete. A very low, uncomfortable-looking bed gave it a cell-like appearance. On the other hand, there was one reasonably comfortable chair, and even two or three old magazines in Serbo-Croat. I went to the door and tried it and found, as I had expected, that Captain Markovic's desire for my co-operation involved locking me in.

I went and sat down and tried to estimate the chances. It might be an unlikely story, but for the life of me I did not see how they could fault it since, up to the time of the crash, all the evidence that they could gather would suggest that I was telling the truth. The fatal flaw was still the period between the crash and when I had telephoned Willie, and the fatal mistake, of course, had been to go back to the hotel. Try as I might to be optimistic, I could not believe that they did not know, or would not find out, about this, and once they knew that I had let over twelve hours elapse between having my passport taken from me at pistol point and reporting it, my whole position as the Injured Husband fell to the ground. I racked my brains for some plausible explanation of how I could have been lying unconscious in the country and in a hotel in Belgrade at one and the same time, but I could think of nothing more convincing than that I must have been concussed by the crash, and have forgotten what happened immediately after it. I decided that this might be worth trying, but it was a forlorn hope.

They brought me some food, which was quite palatable, and as I ate it I looked at my watch and found that it was after two o'clock, so that unless anything had gone wrong, Katherina and Pelic would be safely over the border into Italy. This ought to have cheered me, but for some reason it no longer did. Somehow all the steam and excitement had gone out of things, and I no longer felt like a romantic Scarlet Pimpernel, but merely like somebody who had blundered into serious trouble, and would now probably have to take the consequences.

The time passed very slowly, so that sometimes I thought my watch had stopped, and as time went on the black depression that I usually only felt at night settled down over me. I went and lay down on the bed and tried to sleep, but though I had only had a few hours' uncomfortable sleep the night before, I could do no more than doze fitfully, and when I dozed I suffered from a series of semi-conscious nightmares in which, whilst nothing particularly terrible happened to me, the whole atmosphere varied between acute anxiety and sheer terror. I was forced to wake myself up completely and go and sit in the chair, or walk about the cell. I still remember one of those nightmares. In it, Sarah was telling me about the last few moments before the plane had crashed, and I tried to put out my hand and take hers, and found that my arm was paralysed and would not move. I knew that there were only a few moments during which I could take her hand, and that soon the chance would be gone for ever. But I still could not move my arm, and it was my desperate struggles to do so that woke me up.

I must have been in the cell for seven or eight hours before they came to fetch me. I decided on the way upstairs that I would try the forlorn hope—the story of having wandered about in a daze. Captain Markovic was still sitting at his desk, exactly as I had left him. He gave me a brief nod and silently indicated the chair. As I sat down I said, 'Captain Markovic, whilst I have been waiting, several things have been coming slowly back to me about exactly what happened after my crash, and I think I may unintentionally have misled you.'

'Well?' he said curtly.

'I told you that when I recovered consciousness I looked at my watch and it was half past nine. That is perfectly true. But I realized now that it was still dark, because I had difficulty in seeing the face of my watch. I think it must have been half past nine at night, not half past nine in the morning, which means that instead of being unconscious all night, I can only have been unconscious for quite a short time.'

He nodded again and said, 'Go on.'

'Then several other vague recollections have come back to me. I seem to remember something about the hotel where my wife and I stayed in Belgrade. I must have been concussed or something, because I have no recollection of going there, and I may possibly have dreamed this whole thing. But I seem to recall something about being back in the room that we had had in the hotel and washing the blood off my face. After that there is nothing except a very faint impression that I sat and looked at a river.'

'How long did you sit there?'

'I've no idea. The next thing I remember is that I was going into the Moskva, knowing that I must telephone the Embassy. After that everything is perfectly clear.'

He stared at me for a long time and then looked down at his blotter and said, 'It is very fortunate that these recollections have come back to you. It would have saved a good deal of trouble if they had come back before.' He looked up at me, and the reptilian lips pulled back off the steel teeth and he said, 'Regarding the questions that I am going to ask you, it will be better for everybody, particularly for yourself, if your memory works accurately. . . .' He paused for a moment and then suddenly shot out, 'Where and when did you first meet Pelic?'

I frowned in a puzzled way and said, 'Pelic? Who is Pelic?'

'You don't know the name?'

'No. I don't know anybody of that name.'

'Strange. It is fairly a notorious one. You say this man with whom your wife had the affair called himself Petrov?'

'Yes. Jovan Petrov.'

'Petrov is of course Pelic. Where and when did you first meet him?'

'I've already told you—he introduced himself to us in a restaurant.'

'And he was, naturally, a stranger to your wife also?'

'Oh, yes. At least, as far as I know. She treated him as a stranger.'

'And where and when did you first meet your wife?'

I sensed danger, but there was nothing to be done about it. I said, 'Let me see . . . Yes, it was thirteen years ago at a cocktail party in London.'

'Thirteen years ago at a cocktail party in London,' he said, doing the old comedian's feed act again. He paused and looked around the office, tapping on his blotter with his fingers, as though uncertain what to say next. I thought for a moment that he was baffled, but instead he leaned forward and quietly placed the ace of trumps on the table. He said gently, 'And where and when did you first meet Katherina Feldic?'

That was the one thing I had not been prepared for, and I hesitated. But there was nothing to do now but to go through with it so I said, 'Katherina Feldic? I don't think I know anybody of that name.'

He said, 'Cast back in your memory. It may save a great deal of time and trouble.'

I said thoughtfully, 'Katherina Feldic . . . the name rings a bell somehow. Ah—I have it. I went to a party in Paris not long ago and was introduced to a girl with a name something like that.'

'Exactly.' He suddenly produced a photograph and

thrust it across to me and said, 'Is that Katherina Feldic?'

It was not a very good photograph, and it might have been of either of them but I took the chance and said, 'No, you're getting mixed up. This is a photograph of my wife.'

'Then, what does Katherina Feldic look like?'

'I really can't remember. I only saw her for a few moments.'

'But you admit that this is the woman with whom you have been going about in Belgrade?'

'Of course I admit it. It's my wife.'

Markovic hesitated for just a second, and I guessed that he was really slightly less confident than he sounded. He might be morally certain that it was Katherina who had been with me in Belgrade, but he still had to prove it. I said, 'It looks to me as though there has been some ridiculous muddle somewhere. What makes you think that that photograph is of Katherina what's her name?'

'We know it is.'

'But I said it was a photograph of my wife. Surely you will allow me to know what my own wife looks like? But anyhow what should I be doing in Belgrade with somebody whom I've only ever met for a few seconds?'

His thin lips rolled back from his teeth, and he said harshly, 'You don't seem to realize the seriousness of your position. Aiding and abetting a person in entering Yugoslavia with a false passport is a penal offence, rendering you liable to a long term of imprisonment. If you care to be frank with us we may deal leniently with you. Otherwise you must take the consequences.'

I was rather pleased with this. It confirmed my impression that he was not too sure of his ground. I said, 'Very well. I have nothing to hide. What can I tell you that I haven't told you already?'

'You admit that the woman you were travelling with was Katherina Feldic?'

'I admit nothing of the kind. There are half a dozen people in Paris who would confirm that the woman I was travelling with was my wife. Anyhow, if I wasn't travelling with my wife, where is she?'

That shook him slightly. I pursued my advantage and said, 'You still haven't answered my previous question —why should I have done all this?'

'I was about to ask you that question myself. Why did you do it? Money?'

I laughed, and pulled out my book of travellers' cheques and tossed it across to him. I said, 'I think you will find there's about thirty thousand dollars there. It came from my bank in Beverly Hills, California, when I left the United States, and if you'd like to check you'll find that that money came from an American film company. It doesn't look as though I was exactly short of money, does it?'

Markovic took the book of travellers' cheques and glanced at it closely and then tossed it back to me. He said irritably, 'All this is simply a waste of time. I assure you that we know far more about this affair than you think. We have been very patient with you, but I warn you that that patience is wearing thin. If you will not co-operate with us voluntarily, then we have means of making you do so. I advise you not to force us to use them.'

That made me certain that he wasn't sure of his ground. I said, 'You mean hitting me with rubber clubs or something of that kind? Because I'll remind you that I am a British citizen, and that I have friends at the Embassy who know I am in Belgrade. I was on my way to an appointment at the Embassy when your men picked me up and brought me here. They'll already be wondering what happened to me. It would be a pity if there were a diplomatic incident just because your people have made a mistake somewhere and won't admit it.'

He made no reply but simply rang the bell and said, 'Take him away.'

I rose and said, 'I demand to see somebody from the British Embassy.'

Markovic said, 'Good-bye, Mr. Petersen. Whenever you feel like being more helpful, ask to see me again.'

They took me downstairs, and the first thing I noticed was that the chair had been removed from the cell. I was mildly amused, because it seemed such a childish gesture of rather impotent anger. But the results were not in fact amusing, for it meant that one was forced to sit or lie on the bed, which was very uncomfortable. The food, too, when it came was much poorer and more scanty than before. There was no sign of the rubber club element. I had never supposed that there would be. But there was no doubt that the screws were quietly being put on. I sat down on the bed and smoked a cigarette, and realized that it was my last one, and that again was going to be a serious deprivation. I comforted myself by the reflection that I had done pretty well in my interview with Markovic. It had been a serious blow that he appeared to know all about Katherina. But even so he still could not prove anything, and certainly not that I had been a party to the escape of Pelic, which I suspected was the thing that interested him most. There was also the hope that Willie Strang would have been concerned about my failure to arrive for our meeting, and that he would try to find out what had happened to me. But Willie was not exactly a reliable person and he might very easily forget that we ever made the date, or assume quite blithely that I had simply left Belgrade without telling him that I was going.

There was no means of switching off the neon light from within the cell, so it remained on all night, and that combined with the narrowness and lumpiness of the bed put paid to any chances of real sleep. I remember thinking with bitter self-contempt that one had become a complete slave to Beverly Hills' style comfort. People had only got to take away a chair, and leave one with no cigarettes and no drinks, and make it difficult to sleep, and cut the food down to the bare essentials, and one was almost in desperation within a few hours. All this and so much worse had happened during the war, and yet one had put up with it, and even in a strange way enjoyed it. But that was twenty years ago, and in the meantime one had become soft and flabby and no good as a fighter.

I think the main trouble was a sense of anti-climax. As long as Katherina had been in danger, there had been something to fight for. But now that she was presumably all right, and all that was left was to get out of my own difficulties, the whole thing hardly seemed worth while. I even considered going to Markovic and simply telling him exactly what had happened, and leaving them to do what they liked about it. But somehow I could not bring myself to such a surrender without putting up more of a fight. It might come to that in the end, but not yet.

As the cell was underground, and with no window, and as the neon light was always on, there was nothing to mark the passage of time except by my watch and the coming of my meals. I asked the man who brought the food whether I could have something to read, but he either could not understand English or pretended not to do so, and nothing happened. The food had deteriorated and become scantier, until now it was no more than a plate of thin soup.

But I was never hungry. I have always been able to sleep, after a fashion, anywhere and in any circumstances, and it stood me in good stead now. For whilst there was no question of any long or deep sleep, I spent a lot of my time lying on the bed half waking and half sleeping, and dreaming interminable dreams, all with the same unpleasant, irrational atmosphere. The only other breaks in the twenty-four hours were my meals, which came with great regularity at 8 a.m., 1 p.m. and 7 p.m., and when they came I was allowed to go to the lavatory. I asked to be allowed to wash and shave, but here again I met the blank wall of incomprehension. My most vivid recollection is of an occasion when I really did go properly to sleep, and woke with that curious feeling that I had been asleep a long time. I looked at my watch, and found that it had stopped, and I shall never forget the moment of sheer cold panic as I thought that I did not know what the time was, or whether it was night or day. Why should it have mattered so much I do not know, since it didn't really make very much difference to me. But it most certainly mattered a lot. I had forgotten that I had to be fed, and that even if they would not tell me the time, I should be able to guess it from that, since my watch was going again now, and there were five hours between the first meal and the second one and seven hours between the second and third.

I am still not sure how long things went on like this. I think it was five days, but it may only have been four. By that time, as far as I was concerned, the worst was over. I had not gone mad, as I had thought I might during the first forty-eight hours or so, but had fallen into a sort of dull apathy of acceptance. There was no longer any question of asking to see Markovic, or making a fuss to get some books, or planning to escape when I was allowed to go to the lavatory, or indeed of doing anything else active. Insofar as I wanted anything, it was to be allowed to lie on my bed and doze, and even the coming of my meals, far from being a treat or a relief, had become a sort of intrusion into the special world which I was building for myself. For in that world I could have Sarah whenever I wanted her, and take her where I wanted. I had only to close my eyes and she was there talking to me, and we were in Hollywood or Paris or London or Venice or wherever I chose. Sometimes we had mild rows in our normal way, but strangely enough we very seldom made love. The whole thing had a curious lazy listless atmosphere about it. This was probably because I was becoming rather weak for lack of food, but it was far from unpleasant. Certainly I was closer to her in those rather light-headed waking dreams than I had been at any time since her death. I don't think I ever thought about Katherina after the first day. That chapter was closed and there was no more to be said or even felt about it.

15

On about the sixth day Markovic came to see me, looking more like the usual idea of a civil servant than ever. I was irritated at being aroused from a particularly pleasant dream about Sarah in Italy, but I realized that he would not have come unless he was dissatisfied with the way things were going, which pleased me. Markovic said, 'Well, now, Mr. Petersen, have you anything to say to me?'

I was feeling very weak and listless, but I pulled myself together, and said angrily, 'Yes. I have a lot to say to you. I want to know why I'm being kept here in solitary confinement, on prison food, without even a chance to wash myself. . . .'

Markovic waved a hand and said, 'The business of washing is the result of an oversight. That will be put right.'

'Good. But why am I being kept here at all and refused the chance to talk to my Embassy when no charge is being made against me? I thought you'd got rid of that sort of thing in Yugoslavia long ago.'

'It has been necessary to keep you here purely because of your own obstinacy. As I told you from the start, if you had been prepared to co-operate with us and tell us the truth it would have saved a great deal of time and trouble for everybody, and would also have allowed us to take a more lenient view of what you have done. As it is, we have been forced to keep you here whilst we completed our investigations.'

I said, 'And are they complete now?'

'Virtually, yes. There are merely one or two details which we should still like filled in. In regard to these you can still help us and save time, and I can only say to you, Mr. Petersen, it would pay you handsomely to do so.'

'What are the details?'

'Well, for example—where is your wife?'

'How should I know? With Petrov or Pelic or whatever his name is, presumably.'

'Pelic is in Paris—with Katherina Feldic of course. We know all about their movements. She has taken Pelic to the house in which she usually lives, and they have been about together and seen various Yugoslav émigrés and so on.'

This was a blow. I had forgotten that once back in Paris Katherina would of course start to live what was unmistakably her own life. Markovic saw me hesitate and said, 'I assure you, Mr. Petersen, that this pretence that Katherina Feldic was your wife is now completely exploded. The next detail—did you know, when you brought Katherina Feldic here, that the object was to get Pelic out of the country?'

'I've already told you I'd never heard of Pelic until you mentioned him.'

'That could conceivably be true. Then what was your motive for coming at all? You say that you are not short of money and that it was not that that attracted you. What did?' As I was silent he added, 'Not that it is so very important, but it interests us.'

I said doggedly, 'We came here on holiday.' But I was very tired, and I knew that the game was up now.

Markovic said, 'Then again—and this *is* important from your own point of view. Did you actively aid and abet Pelic to escape, or were you misled by Feldic?'

I said, 'I am prepared to swear that he took my passport from me at pistol point.'

He nodded and said, 'Here again I'm inclined to believe you. A Luger pistol and some surgical tape were found in the house where all this took place. But how did it come about, Mr. Petersen, that when you were arrested you were wearing the raincoat which later inquiries show belonged to Pelic?'

I said, 'Yes—he made me change hats and coats with him when he took my passport. He wanted to look as much like me as possible.'

Markovic bowed his head again, and I could see that he had bought that one. But I was sick of the whole thing by now. Markovic could see that and he rolled what ought to have been his lips back off the steel teeth in what he used for a smile and said, 'Come now, Mr. Petersen—you're a man of sense. Pelic and Katherina Feldic are in Paris, doubtless enjoying themselves. If that's the result you wanted it has been achieved. But in order to achieve it you have been left in our hands, and we can prove that you have not only lied to us, but acted illegally and against the interests of this country. It is quite useless to talk about appealing to your Embassy. They would be the first to tell you that they can do nothing for you. A visitor to this country— or indeed any other country—must obey the law of the land or take the consequences. *We* are the only people who can help you now—if you help us. Now—for the last time—why did you bring Katherina Feldic to Belgrade?'

I think if he had been only a trifle more *simpatico*, I should have told him the whole story. But I hated to throw my hand in to a man like Markovic, and while I was hesitating it suddenly occurred to me that I could not tell the story of the gold and the jewellery without implicating Katherina's grandfather and grandmother, and that, somehow, was unthinkable. I said dully, 'I keep telling you—we came here on holiday,' and then added, 'After all—haven't you ever taken a pretty girl anywhere?'

It was said purely as an afterthought but Markovic looked up sharply and I realized that he was interested. He said keenly, 'You mean that you brought her here —purely as a mistress?'

'Why else?'

I saw a last chance and rapidly redeployed my forces. I said, 'Look, Captain Markovic, I may as well tell you the truth. I met Katherina Feldic in Paris and fell for her. I wanted to take her away with me somewhere, and she suggested Belgrade because she hadn't been here since she was a child. Like a fool, I agreed to bring her, using my wife's passport. The rest you know. That was why I was so anxious that you should think she was my wife, because I wanted to avoid any scandal.'

There was a long silence, and then Markovic heaved a sigh which may or may not have been one of relief and said, 'You have been very wise, Mr. Petersen, to tell me that. You have, as you say, been foolish. But foolishness is one thing, and conspiracy against the state quite another. I shall now submit my report to higher quarters, and I am afraid we're to keep you here till we know their decision. But in the meantime we can perhaps make you a little more comfortable.'

I said, 'How long will they be making up their minds?'

He shrugged his shoulders and said, 'I'm afraid I can't say. From this afternoon the matter is out of my hands. Good-bye, Mr. Petersen. I probably shan't see you again. In case I do not, good luck.'

I said, 'Thank you, Captain Markovic.' He went out and closed the door behind him and then immediately opened it again and put his head in and said, 'Forgive me, but just one more thing—my first detail question. Where is your wife now?'

I said, 'My wife is dead.'

He nodded and said, 'Yes. According to our information, she was killed in an air crash recently. Is that so?'

'Yes.'

He nodded again and said, 'I'm glad to have that confirmed. I commiserate with you. Good-bye, Mr. Petersen.'

The first thing they did was to bring the chair back. It made a surprising difference; for whereas before all I could do was to lie on my bed and drift into a fantasy world, I could now sit in the chair and think. I considered my last talk with Markovic and decided that it might have been worse. I had now confessed to an illegal action in bringing Katherina to Yugoslavia, which I had not done before. But this was only telling them what they already knew beyond doubt. Meanwhile, I seemed to have satisfied Markovic about my motives for bringing her, so that the question of the gold and jewellery had never arisen, and the old people would not be involved. I also seemed to have satisfied him that I had not aided and abetted the escape of Pelic. I appeared now as the simple soul who had been led into an illegal act by his pretty mistress, and I decided that this was the best I could hope for.

Apart from the return of the chair there were other signs that I was no longer under pressure. I was brought a reasonable meal, for which, rather surprisingly, I had no appetite; and best of all, I was allowed to wash and shave. After a week or so in limbo, life was beginning again, and I remember well sitting in that chair, freshly washed and shaven, after what I could eat of a reasonable meal, and wondering whether I welcomed the change or not. It is a well-known fact that people who suffer from long illnesses often reach the stage where they are reluctant to leave hospital, and that some prisoners dislike leaving prison. They are what the psychologists call 'institutionalized.' They have become used to a way of life, however unpleasant or dull, and to change it involves them in effort which they do not wish to make. I must confess that several times I lay on the bed hoping for my waking dreams of Sarah. But it was no use. Shaved, washed and fed as I was, she would not come to me as she had done before.

They came for me that same evening, but this time I was not taken to Markovic's office but right up to a sort of penthouse on the top of the building and shown into a most curious cross between an office and a drawing-room. It was a big room, and from its windows there was a splendid view over the roof tops of Belgrade. There was a large modern desk with three telephones on it and a swivel desk chair upholstered in leather. The rest was French eighteenth century with a lot of gilt and cabriole legs and a fine Aubusson carpet. My mind went back to the room in Katherina's grandparents' house, with the combination of the blue velvet upholstered furniture, and the grand piano and the night stool.

The man who sat at the desk was an impressive figure. He must have been about sixty, and he had thick, close-cropped grey hair. He was a big man, broad shouldered and deep chested, and he sat upright in his chair as though he was riding a horse. He was wearing the uniform of a general, but his left sleeve was empty and was pinned neatly across the front of his tunic, partly obscuring the rows of medal ribbons on his chest. He had a swarthy brown face and fine dark eyes, so that there seemed to be a touch of the gipsy about him.

My escort gave my name and went out. The general

silently waved me to a chair, and sat looking at me with the dark gipsy eyes, so that for several moments we simply stared at one another in silence. Then he said curtly, 'I have here a report on your behaviour.'

He had a very deep voice, and he said it severely, as a headmaster might speak to an unsatisfactory pupil. He said, 'I understand that you now admit, after a great deal of prevarication, that you brought this woman Katherina Feldic to Yugoslavia with you, pretending that she was your wife, and using your wife's passport?' He spoke English completely fluently, sometimes almost pedantically, using unnecessarily long words, but he had slightly more accent than Markovic.

I said, 'Yes—I have admitted that.'

'You realize, of course, that this was quite illegal?'

'Yes.'

'And that you were committing a serious offence?'

'I realize that it was an offence, but I did not think at the time that it was a very serious one. I thought Miss Feldic wanted to come to Belgrade for purely sentimental reasons.'

'So you have said. You merely wished to come on a holiday with your mistress. But by aiding and abetting her to get into the country under false pretences you were not only committing an offence, but acting against a friendly Yugoslavia. You had been given a visa and the hospitality of the country. This is the way you repay it.'

I said, 'I'm afraid I hadn't thought of it like that. Certainly I have nothing but friendly feelings towards Yugoslavia.'

'And you maintain that you knew nothing of Pelic, and were not privy to any plot to get him out of the country?'

'Certainly not. As I have told Captain Markovic I

only met him for a few minutes under the name of Petrov. The next time I saw him was when he was taking my passport away from me at pistol point.'

The general said, 'So your contention is that, apart from the deliberate offence of bringing her into the country, you were simply an innocent tool of this woman and her ridiculous friends in Paris?'

'That is so.'

He sat and stared at me with the fine brown eyes for a disconcertingly long time and then said, 'I have been trying to give you the benefit of the doubt. You have been very foolish, but it is at least possible that you did not know that you were meddling with dangerous matters and consorting with people who were not to be trusted.'

I said, 'I realize this now.'

He nodded and said, 'I hope you do. As it is, you have committed a grave offence, refused for a long time to co-operate with us, and put us to a great deal of trouble and expense. We should be perfectly justified in bringing you to trial and sending you to prison for a long period. But as we think you have merely been a tool for other people I shall treat you leniently. I believe you are carrying a considerable sum of money with you?'

'Yes.'

'Then you will pay the sum of ten thousand dollars towards the costs of these investigations. The alternative is a formal trial. I strongly advise you to pay the money.'

I said, 'Very well.' There didn't seem to be anything much else to say.

'Apart from that I will give you twenty-four hours to leave Yugoslavia. If you are still in the country after that, you will certainly be arrested.' He stared down at his blotter for a long time and then, looking up, smiled for the first time. He said in his deep-chested voice, 'You are a very lucky man, Mr. Petersen.'

I said, 'I realize that.'

'I do not think you realize quite how lucky. As soon as it is publicly known that Pelic has escaped from the country, it will be a front page news item. I and my department will certainly be criticized in some quarters for having allowed it to happen. If it had been of vital importance to keep Pelic in the country, I could not possibly have treated you so leniently. As it is, you have unwittingly helped us to solve a difficult problem.'

I said, 'What problem?'

'The problem of what to do with Pelic. Here is a man who was not so much a traitor as a public nuisance. After his American upbringing and experience, he simply could not accept the necessity for certain aspects of our system. But he did not go into secret opposition or plot against the Government. He simply openly published his objections and criticisms in an offensive way which no Government could tolerate. He was, in fact, a trouble maker of the most irritating kind. Powerful influences in the Government have long been pressing us simply to get rid of him by putting him in gaol and keeping him there. But Pelic's father was one of the Marshal's oldest and most devoted supporters—a man with a magnificent record in the service of Yugoslavia. He is dead now, but he is remembered with the deepest respect and affection. The Marshal is very loyal to his old friends, and for this reason he has always refused to take a tough line with Pelic, despite various provocations, and strong pressure from the Left Wing of the Party. There will be an outcry at first about his escape, but when that's died down, everyone will realize that he will be far less of a nuisance in Paris than he was in Yugoslavia. Speaking for my own department, we are delighted to see the back of him.'

I said, 'Then why on earth didn't you just give him a passport and tell him to go?'

'Politically speaking, that would have been quite impossible. There would have been a storm of criticism from the Left, who already feel that he has been far too leniently treated. As it is, with your accidental help, he has escaped, which is the perfect solution to the problem. Now, there is nothing anybody can do except to criticize me and my department for our slackness, and that is a thing which we are quite used to.'

I said, 'It seems to me, General, that *you* owe *me* ten thousand dollars.'

He smiled again and said, 'Ah, no—even leniency does not extend that far.' He rang the bell on his desk and rose and held out his hand, which I took. He said, 'Good-bye, Mr. Petersen. You will pay your fine and you will then be released, and you will leave Yugoslavia at once. It has been an expensive visit for you, but perhaps you have learnt something from it.'

My escort appeared, and we were half-way to the door when the general suddenly said, 'Ah, Mr. Petersen—one last thing, since everything is now settled. Why did you *really* bring Katherina Feldic to Yugoslavia?'

I said dully, 'Because she was very like my wife.'

He nodded and said, 'Ah, yes—of course. I quite understand. Good-bye.'

16

THE Embassy rallied round nobly and produced me a new passport at high speed. Even so it was rather more than twenty-four hours after my interview with the general when I took off by plane for Paris. I had no luggage. That had all gone with the car. I managed to find time to buy a few of the absolute essentials like a toothbrush and a razor in Belgrade, but otherwise I was reduced literally to what I stood up in, and, indeed, had slept in for the last week. I had no more than my usual moment of terror as we took off. It seemed that the real cold horror of airplanes and anything connected with them that I felt immediately after Sarah's death had passed.

In the plane I reckoned up what the whole expedition had cost me, and what with the ten thousand dollar fine, the cost of the car, the money I had given Katherina and our ordinary hotel and living expenses it came to just over twenty thousand dollars, and in return I had been double-crossed, held up at gun point, had nearly broken my neck, and had spent about a week in gaol and solitary confinement. Yet for some reason, now that it was all over I did not regret any of these things. My worries were not about what had happened, but about what was to happen now. I was very tired after all the complications of the last fortnight, but even so, the prospect of once more being in Paris with nothing to do was terrifying. I thought at first of trying to find Katherina. I had only a very vague idea of where she lived and had long forgotten her telephone number. But as she had been at

Roy Featherstone's party he presumably knew her, or knew somebody who did. Nevertheless, I put the idea firmly aside. The incident was over, and it was best to draw a line through it and expect no more of it.

The first two days in Paris were not so bad. I was busy replacing my lost clothes and suit-cases, and it was a relief to sleep in a comfortable bed at the St. Jacques and to eat excellent food. But by the third day the ghastly feeling of futility and paralysis began to creep over me again. I almost wished that I had refused to pay the fine and let myself be sent to a Yugoslav gaol. That at least would have been a new experience, whereas sitting alone outside the Café de la Paix was not. On the fourth day I abandoned all my sensible resolutions and rang up Roy Featherstone to see if he could tell me where to find Katherina.

Roy Featherstone was not very helpful. At first he positively denied all knowledge of her. When I reminded him that she had been at his party and that he had introduced us, if not very coherently, he remembered her vaguely and thought she must have come with a couple whose telephone number he gave me. After some difficulty, I contacted them, and they were able to give me what I recognized as her old telephone number. But when I rang this number I was told that she had left the house and was living elsewhere. They could not give me the telephone number, but they gave me the address, which was somewhere which sounded as though it was in Montparnasse.

By this time my need to see her had become a matter of desperate urgency. What I expected, or even wanted, from such a meeting I do not know. I remember telling myself, as an excuse, that it was all to do with Sarah's passport—that it was vital that I should get it back. But it was a lame excuse, and I don't think I ever really believed it. I think perhaps what I really wanted was for her to kiss me again and say, 'Thank you, Jim,' as she had done when we parted in the empty house. But chiefly I just wanted to see that face again.

Reason or no reason, as soon as I knew her address, I took a cab and went over to the Left Bank. We had some difficulty in finding the street, which was long and narrow, and we were moving along it slowly, looking for the number, when Katherina appeared in the doorway of a house about thirty yards ahead of us. She stood for a moment looking back into the house, and in that moment, as we crawled towards her at walking pace, the illusion was almost perfect. Not only the face and the figure and the lovely legs, but the whole set of the body and tilt of the head were there, exactly as I remembered them.

I was leaning forward to call to the driver to stop—to jump out and greet her—when Pelic came out behind her. He was looking extraordinarily handsome, and I could see the curious bright blue of his eyes as they smiled at one another. We were only about ten yards away. I called, 'Stop!' and I remembered that my voice cracked in a curious way as I said the word. We stopped a few yards from them, and then Pelic put his arm around her waist and led her out on to the pavement, and they set off down the street with his arm still around her.

The cab driver said, '*Voici vingt-sept.*'

I said, '*Oui. Un moment . . .*' I sat in the cab and watched them as they walked away down the long narrow street, with Pelic's arm round her waist. Then they turned the corner and disappeared, and I realized with calm, cold grief, that even the last fleeting shadow of Sarah was gone from me for ever. I said, 'I wonder what you would have made of that little episode, darling? I expect you would have been very jealous. But can ashes be jealous?'

The taxi driver turned his head and said inquiringly, '*Alors Monsieur* . . . ?'

It was the vital, the unanswerable question—'Now what?' But some attempt had to be made at answering it, however feebly, because I was alive and sitting in a taxi, and if one is sitting in a taxi, one is presumably going somewhere. So I told him to drive to the Air France offices, and booked myself a ticket for an evening flight to London.